RR

DATE DUE

What looked like fireflies winked in the darkness surrounding the camp, but Fargo knew those flashes of light didn't come from harmless insects. They were muzzle flashes of guns as night riders attacked the wagon train.

Fargo pulled the Henry rifle from its sheath as he galloped closer. Suddenly a rider veered toward him out of the darkness and motioned for him to rein in. The man held a revolver in his hand, and a spray of silvery moonlight revealed a bandanna across his face. He called in a muffled voice, "Damn, they're putting up one hell of a fight!" Suddenly he realized that Fargo wasn't wearing a mask.

"Hey, you're not one of us!" The gun in his hand jerked toward Fargo.

"That's right, I'm not," Fargo said, and fired the Henry into the outlaw at point-blank range. . . .

THE

TRAILSMAN

#282

KANSAS WEAPON WOLVES

by

Jon Sharpe

A SIGNET BOOK

SIGNET
Published by New American Library, a division of
Penguin Group (USA) Inc., 375 Hudson Street,
New York, New York 10014, USA
Penguin Group (Canada), 10 Alcorn Avenue, Toronto,
Ontario M4V 3B2, Canada (a division of Pearson Penguin Canada Inc.)
Penguin Books Ltd., 80 Strand, London WC2R 0RL, England
Penguin Ireland, 25 St. Stephen's Green, Dublin 2,
Ireland (a division of Penguin Books Ltd.)
Penguin Group (Australia), 250 Camberwell Road, Camberwell, Victoria 3124,
Australia (a division of Pearson Australia Group Pty. Ltd.)
Penguin Books India Pvt. Ltd., 11 Community Centre, Panchsheel Park,
New Delhi - 110 017, India
Penguin Group (NZ), cnr Airborne and Rosedale Roads, Albany,
Auckland 1310, New Zealand (a division of Pearson New Zealand Ltd.)
Penguin Books (South Africa) (Pty.) Ltd., 24 Sturdee Avenue,
Rosebank, Johannesburg 2196, South Africa

Penguin Books Ltd., Registered Offices:
80 Strand, London WC2R 0RL, England

First published by Signet, an imprint of New American Library,
a division of Penguin Group (USA) Inc.

First Printing, April 2005
10 9 8 7 6 5 4 3 2 1

The first chapter of this book previously appeared in *New Mexico Nightmare,*
the two hundred eighty-first volume in this series.

Copyright © Penguin Group (USA) Inc., 2005
All rights reserved

 REGISTERED TRADEMARK—MARCA REGISTRADA

PUBLISHER'S NOTE
This is a work of fiction. Names, characters, places, and incidents either are
the product of the author's imagination or are used fictitiously, and any resemblance to actual persons, living or dead, business establishments, events, or
locales is entirely coincidental.

The Trailsman

Beginnings . . . they bend the tree and they mark the man. Skye Fargo was born when he was eighteen. Terror was his midwife, vengeance his first cry. Killing spawned Skye Fargo, ruthless, cold-blooded murder. Out of the acrid smoke of gunpowder still hanging in the air, he rose, cried out a promise never forgotten.

The Trailsman they began to call him all across the West: searcher, scout, hunter, the man who could see where others only looked, his skills for hire but not his soul, the man who lived each day to the fullest, yet trailed each tomorrow. Skye Fargo, the Trailsman, the seeker who could take the wildness of a land and the wanting of a woman and make them his own.

Kansas Territory, 1860—
where parched ground is watered,
not by rain but by the blood of innocents.

1

For a town, the City of Kansas wasn't bad, thought the big man in buckskins as he rode along the main street, sitting easily in the saddle on the back of the magnificent black-and-white Ovaro stallion. Skye Fargo preferred being out on the frontier, far from civilization, but settlements *did* have their advantages.

Fargo was looking at one of them right now.

His lake-blue eyes lingered appreciatively on the ripe curves of a young woman with long, honey-colored hair as she stood on the driver's box of a big wagon. She was supervising the loading of crates into the wagon from a warehouse alongside the Missouri River.

"Let's go!" she called, hurrying the laborers who were hauling the crates. "There are people starving in Kansas!"

Fargo reined in and rested his hands on the pommel of his saddle, easing his back after the long ride across Missouri from St. Louis. He was on his way to Kansas, so he was interested in the young woman's comment about people starving there.

Fargo knew that a year and a half earlier a drought had settled down over Kansas Territory that remained unbroken. The lack of rain had dried up the land and ruined crops, but he hadn't heard that things were so bad people were starving.

That was certainly possible, though, he told himself.

Some folks referred to the broad expanse of flatland in the middle of the country as The Great American Desert. Fargo knew that wasn't true; he had crossed enough real deserts to know the difference.

But the prairie could be mighty inhospitable when the weather was too dry, as it had been for the past eighteen months. Clearly it was getting worse.

The wagon being loaded in front of the warehouse was only one vehicle in a line of wagons. As Fargo watched a man came along the line talking to the drivers. He was short, broad, and muscular, with a red face and fair hair under a broad-brimmed black hat. He carried a curled bullwhip and tapped it against his thigh as he walked.

When he reached the wagon where the young woman was, he asked, "About done, Sallie?"

She nodded and said, "Yes, Pa. I'll pull forward as soon as the men are finished."

So they were father and daughter. Fargo could see the resemblance now. And the young woman was the driver of that rig, an unusual job for a female.

Sallie looked like she could handle it, though. She wore boots, a brown canvas divided skirt, a gray woolen shirt, and a buckskin vest. A brown hat hung behind her head by its chin strap.

She also had a cartridge belt strapped around her waist, with the walnut grips of a revolver jutting up from the holster attached to it. A shotgun lay on the floorboards at her feet. She was ready for trouble if it came calling.

Her father nodded and moved on to the wagons ahead of her in line. They had already been loaded, Fargo saw, and now men were snugging down canvas covers over their cargoes.

Fargo had seen enough supply trains to recognize one when he came across it. He had even guided similar trains across the plains on several occasions in his adventurous career as a guide, scout, and trailblazer. He wondered where this one was bound.

He might have stopped and talked to the burly, fair-haired man, who was probably the wagon master, but he was tired and so was the Ovaro. They had been in St. Louis when the message caught up to him, asking him to come to Topeka, Kansas Territory, as soon as possible to discuss a business proposition with a man named Henry Coleman.

Fargo didn't know Coleman, but the man had enclosed a hundred-dollar bank note to show that he was serious and to pay for Fargo's time and trouble. Since Fargo didn't have anything else on his plate at the moment, he had bought some supplies and headed west. Topeka was still a two to three day ride beyond the settlement at the junction of the Kansas and Missouri Rivers that called itself the City of Kansas.

Heeling the Ovaro into motion, Fargo started past the wagons, intending to find first a hotel and then a saloon. He hadn't gone very far, however, when a commotion erupted behind him.

Fargo reined in again and turned in the saddle to see that a fistfight had broken out between a couple of roughly dressed men. One of the combatants was a driver from the wagon train. The other looked to be a cowboy.

Whatever had provoked the fight was their business and none of his, Fargo told himself. He needed a drink, a hot meal, maybe a few hands of poker to relax, and a good place to sleep. He didn't need to get mixed up in some fracas.

But then the young woman with honey-colored hair jumped down from her wagon and ran toward the fight, and Fargo had to watch and see what was going to happen.

The cowboy had friends and so did the teamster. The two groups converged to watch the fight, and a lot of hostile stares were exchanged. But no one was throwing any punches yet except the two men who had started the fight.

Fargo had a good view from the back of the Ovaro. He could see over the heads of the men gathered around the brawlers. The two men slugged away at each other, raising a small cloud of dust as their feet scuffed back and forth in the street.

Sallie pushed her way through the other men from the wagon train, not being shy about using her elbows to make a path. She broke out of the crowd just as the cowboy landed the most solid blow yet, a hard, looping right that caught the teamster on the jaw and knocked him sprawling on his back. A cheer went up from the cowboy's friends.

If it had ended there, that would have been one thing. But the cowboy wasn't willing to let it end. He stepped forward quickly and swung his leg in a brutal kick that sent the toe of his boot crashing into the teamster's ribs. The man on the ground let out a sharp cry of pain.

"Leave him alone!" Sallie yelled as she threw herself at the cowboy's back.

She grabbed him, but he broke loose, spun around, and swung his left arm in a vicious backhand. The blow landed on Sallie's face and sent her stumbling backward a couple of steps before she fell.

"Damn!" Fargo muttered. He couldn't let that pass.

Turning the Ovaro, he sent the stallion surging toward the crowd. With startled yells, men got out of the way of the big black-and-white horse. The crowd parted and let Fargo through, and as he reached the circle in which the two men had fought he swung down from the saddle.

The cowboy was about to rejoin his friends, not

paying any further attention to the young woman after he had knocked her down. He stopped, though, when one of the other men said, "Uh-oh, Brinker, looks like trouble comin'."

Brinker turned and glowered at the big, buckskin-clad man approaching him. It was apparent at first glance that Fargo was no teamster. He was lithe and muscular, with thick dark hair and a close-cropped dark beard. A holstered Colt revolver rode easily on his right hip, and the wooden haft of an Arkansas Toothpick stuck up from a fringed sheath strapped to his right calf. It was obvious that Fargo knew how to use those weapons, too.

"Back off, mister," Brinker said. "This ain't your fight."

"It wasn't," Fargo agreed, "until you knocked down that young woman."

"She shouldn't have jumped me! When she grabbed me I didn't know but what it was another one o' them holy joes lookin' for a fight."

Sallie had pushed herself to her knees by now. She stood up the rest of the way and brushed dust from her skirt. "No one from our wagon train is looking for a fight!"

Brinker pointed at the man he had battered down and kicked. "What about him?" he demanded. "He started the ruckus!"

Sallie bent over the man and began helping him to his feet. He held himself awkwardly, probably because that kick might have cracked one of his ribs.

"Is that true, Matt?" Sallie asked him.

"I . . . I don't know what the big galoot's talkin' about, Miss Sallie," the man said, his voice taut with pain. "I was just sittin' on my wagon when this fella came along and said I spit on his boot."

"You did!" Brinker insisted.

"I never did no such thing! You got me mixed up with somebody else, mister."

"It was him," one of the other cowboys said. "We all saw it, didn't we, boys?"

Nods and mutters of agreement came from the men with him.

"I don't care about any of that," Fargo said flatly as he faced Brinker. "You assaulted that young woman. Apologize."

Brinker sneered at him. "Who appointed you the protector of the fair flower of womanhood, hombre?"

Sallie took a step toward Fargo. "It's all right, you don't have to defend me, sir. I appreciate it, but it's not necessary."

Fargo turned his head toward her. "I just don't like to see anybody mistreating a lady—"

It was at that moment, from the corner of his eye, that he saw Brinker lunge toward him, swinging a big knobby fist.

Fargo's instincts took over, pulling him sharply to the side so that Brinker's punch missed him for the most part, barely grazing his right ear instead of landing squarely in his face. Fargo struck back, jabbing a right straight ahead. The punch packed plenty of power despite traveling only a short distance. His fist sunk into Brinker's belly almost to the wrist.

Brinker grunted as breath sour with the stink of raw whiskey gusted out of his mouth. He stumbled forward, but as he did so his arms went out and wrapped around Fargo in a bear hug that couldn't be avoided. Brinker twisted and drove Fargo back against the side of one of the wagons.

That impact caused Fargo to lose what little air he had been able to trap in his lungs when Brinker grabbed him. He knew he wouldn't be able to hold out for very long unless he could break the grip the cowboy had on him.

He tried to bring a knee up into Brinker's groin, but Brinker twisted at the hips and took the blow on his thigh. Fargo couldn't work an arm loose, so that left him with only one choice.

He lowered his head and butted Brinker in the face as hard as he could.

Brinker howled as the head-butt pulped his nose and made blood shoot from his nostrils. He let go of Fargo and stumbled backward, lifting both hands to his nose as crimson welled from it and covered the lower half of his face.

Fargo didn't give him time to recover. He waded in, throwing a left to the belly that made Brinker drop his hands again and uncover his face. As soon as Fargo saw that opening, he sent a right uppercut whistling in to land solidly on Brinker's jaw. The cowboy's feet came off the ground and a second later he crashed down in the street on his back.

He didn't move after that, just lay there giving off a soft, bubbling moan.

"Get that son of a bitch!" yelled one of Brinker's friends. The group of cowboys started to surge forward toward Fargo.

A sharp cracking sound stopped them in their tracks.

They must have thought it was a gunshot, but Fargo knew better. He wasn't surprised when the burly wagon master he had seen earlier stepped forward, his bullwhip uncoiled now. Like the blacksnake that was its namesake, the whip hissed and writhed in the dust at the man's feet.

"That's enough!" the man bellowed. "There'll be no more fighting!" He turned toward the young woman. "Sallie, are you all right?"

"I'm fine, Pa," she told him. "But I think Matt here might have a broken rib."

"Is that right, Matt?"

The injured man grimaced as he nodded. "I'm afraid so, Mr. McCabe. It sure hurts when I move or take a breath."

"We'll find a doctor to take a look at you. Reckon you'll be able to handle your team if those ribs are bandaged up tightly enough?"

"Don't know, but I'll sure try."

McCabe slapped him on the shoulder, which made Matt wince again. "Good man," the wagon master boomed. He motioned to one of the other drivers. "Saul, take Matt here and see if you can find a sawbones."

"Yes, sir, Mr. McCabe," the second driver said.

As they moved off down the street, Matt walking gingerly and slowly, McCabe turned to Fargo and said, "I saw what happened, sir. I appreciate you coming to the defense of my daughter."

"I could have taken care of this trouble myself," Sallie put in.

Fargo smiled. "Like I said, I won't stand for a lady being manhandled." He glanced at the group of cowboys, who had helped Brinker to his feet and then withdrawn a short distance. They were still muttering among themselves and casting an occasional baleful glance in Fargo's direction.

"I appreciate it, too," Sallie said, "but I can take care of myself."

McCabe smiled at Fargo. "Don't mind her, she's always been a feisty one." He stuck out his hand. "Joshua McCabe, sir, at your service. I'm the leader of this wagon train."

Fargo shook McCabe's hand and introduced himself. "They call me Skye Fargo."

8

"The one who's sometimes known as the Trailsman?" McCabe asked, his eyes narrowing slightly.

Fargo shrugged and nodded. He had long since accepted the fact that some people would know him by the nickname that had been hung on him. "That's right."

"I've heard of you. You're said to be the best guide on the frontier."

Fargo could see McCabe's eyes practically light up with the idea that occurred to him. That didn't come as a surprise to Fargo, either.

McCabe went on. "Perhaps I could discuss a little business with you, Mr. Fargo."

"Sorry, I've already got places to go and things to do," Fargo replied. "I just stopped for a minute because I didn't like the way that fracas was going."

"But surely you could hear me out!" McCabe insisted. "That wouldn't do any harm. Over supper, say, at Wellman's Restaurant? You must eat, Mr. Fargo."

"I do like to eat," Fargo admitted with a faint smile. And Wellman's had probably the best steaks in this part of Missouri, he added to himself.

"It's settled then. In an hour at Wellman's?"

"All right, on one condition," Fargo said.

"What's that?"

"That Miss Sallie here joins us."

"Of course," McCabe agreed, even though Sallie looked a little dubious about the idea.

She said, "I don't know if we'll be finished loading by then . . ."

"The men can finish without us," McCabe interrupted her. "We'll be there, Mr. Fargo."

"No promises about that business you want to talk about," Fargo said. "In fact, I can tell you now that I already have another job offer lined up."

"Who said anything about a job?" McCabe began

coiling his whip. Brinker and his friends had disappeared into one of the nearby saloons by now. "I'd just like to buy you dinner to thank you for your help, that's all."

"Uh-huh," Fargo said. He didn't believe that for a second.

But he wasn't going to turn down a free steak at Wellman's, especially when he could enjoy it in the company of a young woman as pretty as Sallie McCabe.

Fargo rented a room for the night in a decent but not too expensive hotel and stabled the Ovaro in a barn in back of the place. By the time he had put his gear in his room and stepped back out onto the boardwalk in front of the hotel, the sun was going down. It was still a little early to be heading for Wellman's Restaurant, so he decided to have a quick drink first.

The nearest saloon was called the Great Plains Palace. When Fargo walked in he saw that it was doing a decent business, but it was still too early for the saloon to be really crowded. He strolled over to the bar and signaled to a red-jacketed bartender.

"Whiskey," Fargo told the man. The bartender poured the drink and deftly scooped up the coin Fargo tossed onto the bar.

Before Fargo could lift the glass to his mouth, a big, rough hand clapped him on the shoulder. He reacted instinctively, pivoting toward whoever had grabbed him. His hand dropped to the butt of the Colt on his hip.

"Whoa!" said the man who had come up behind Fargo. He stepped back and raised both hands, palms out to show that he meant no harm. "Take it easy, Skye. It's just me."

Fargo found himself looking into a familiar bushy-bearded face. The man had a tangled thatch of black hair under a broad-brimmed felt hat with a high, round crown. He wore buckskins like Fargo's, and his rather homely face split in a broad grin that made it less ugly.

"Damn it, Reuben," Fargo said, "that's a good way to get yourself killed!"

"Yeah, I know," the big man called Reuben rumbled. "I was just so glad to see you that I didn't think. It's been a while since our trails crossed."

That was true enough. It had been two years since he had seen Reuben Sanborn, Fargo thought. That was in . . . Santa Fe, that was it. They had found themselves in a brawl in a cantina and had fought back to back until all their enemies were sprawled around them, moaning in pain and unable to move. Fargo liked to think of himself as a peaceable man, but he enjoyed a good fight from time to time, and that had been a good one.

"What are you doing here?" Fargo asked as he motioned for his old friend to join him at the bar.

"I'm at loose ends," Reuben replied. "Been doin' a little trapping up in the Tetons, but the season's over and I decided to find me a good place to spend the winter. I was thinkin' about ridin' on over to St. Louis."

"How many years has it been since you spent more than a week at a time in a town?"

The mountain man chuckled. "Well, it's been a spell, I'll grant you that. But I'm gettin' older, Skye. It's about time I started thinkin' about settlin' down."

Fargo shook his head. "That'll be the day."

"Yeah, you're probably right," Reuben agreed. He crooked a finger at the bartender and pantomimed throwing back a shot of whiskey. While the bartender was pouring the drink, Reuben went on. "What are you doing here, Skye?"

"I'm on my way to Topeka, over in Kansas Territory."

"On business?"

"Maybe. I don't know for sure yet."

"You were always on the move." Reuben downed the drink that the bartender set in front of him and smacked his lips in satisfaction. "You're just about the most fiddle-footed gent I ever saw, Skye Fargo."

"I reckon I come by it natural," Fargo said with a shrug.

"How about we get some supper?" Reuben suggested.

"Sorry, I can't. I've already got a dinner engagement."

Another grin wreathed Reuben's bushy features. "With a pretty little gal, I'll bet."

"*And* her father."

"Oh? Well, that's different. When you're done, why don't you come back here? We'll chew the fat, maybe play some cards, kill a bottle or two of Who-Hit-John."

"It's a deal," Fargo said.

He shook hands with the burly mountain man and then left the Great Plains Palace, heading for the restaurant. He was glad he had run into Reuben Sanborn. Fargo had friends scattered all across the West, men he might not encounter except every two or three years, but he was always happy to see them.

It had been a little early for the saloon trade, but it was just the right time for the dinner hour. Wellman's was crowded. Joshua McCabe and his daughter Sallie had arrived first and had gotten a table. They spotted each other as Fargo came into the restaurant, and McCabe lifted a hand in greeting.

As he went over to join them, Fargo saw that they had changed clothes. McCabe wore a sober black suit, and instead of her rougher, more functional garb Sallie wore a light-blue gown with white lace around the square-cut neckline. The dress made her look younger, softer, and prettier, though Fargo had thought she was very attractive when he saw her earlier.

McCabe stood up to shake hands and said, "Sit down, Mr. Fargo. We're glad you could join us."

"My pleasure," Fargo said. He smiled at Sallie as he sat down across from her and added, "I see you're not sporting a six-shooter anymore."

"No, but I have a derringer in my handbag," she returned with a smile of her own.

"Sallie!" her father scolded her. "Mr. Fargo's going to think you're some sort of wild woman."

"I just believe in being prepared."

"Well, you won't need a gun in here."

Fargo thought that was probably right—Wellman's was a nice place—but on the frontier you could never entirely rule out the chance of needing a gun. A fella never knew what might happen.

"You carry around a bullwhip," Sallie pointed out.

"I didn't bring it with me tonight," McCabe said. "Besides, a whip isn't the same as a gun."

"A man can be whipped to death, just like he can be shot." Sallie looked at Fargo. "Isn't that true, Mr. Fargo?"

"Sad to say, it is," Fargo agreed. "I've seen men whipped to death."

Sallie's eyes widened. She had been arguing with her father because she liked to argue, Fargo sensed. She hadn't expected him to back her up with the evidence of his own eyes.

"You have?" she said.

Fargo nodded. "It's not anything I'd want to see again, either."

"Well, of course not," McCabe said. "Please, let's

talk about something a little less, ah, gruesome, shall we?"

Fargo obliged by asking, "Where are you folks from?"

"Indiana," McCabe replied. "When our church heard about the plight of all those poor people suffering from the drought in Kansas, we decided to get together with other congregations from all over the Midwest and send some supplies. I was chosen to head the expedition since I had some experience as a freighter before I became a man of the cloth."

"You're a preacher?"

McCabe nodded. "I'm the pastor of our church."

That came as something of a surprise to Fargo, since McCabe didn't seem much like a minister to him. But the Good Lord called all sorts of folks to do His work, Fargo supposed, even burly wagon masters who could wield a bullwhip with an expert hand. He remembered, too, that Brinker had referred to the people with the supply wagons as "holy joes." That comment made sense now.

A waiter came up to the table then and took their orders. While they were waiting for their food, McCabe explained more about the effort to provide help for the settlers in Kansas.

"All the supplies were shipped here to the City of Kansas by rail and stored in a warehouse until we could get here with the wagons. They're loaded now and we're ready to pull out first thing in the morning."

Fargo frowned. "I hope you've got guards posted on those wagons tonight. With supplies so scarce across the river, what you're carrying could be worth quite a bit of money."

"Yes, of course we thought of that. I asked several of our drivers to stand guard tonight. I don't think anyone would try to steal the wagons right here in the middle of town."

"You never know," Fargo said. "Some hombres will do almost anything if they think they can make some money out of the deal."

"We'll be careful, don't worry. I'm more concerned about the trip from here to Topeka. Lawrence is the only good-sized settlement along the way, and there's a lot of open territory where bandits could attack the wagons. It'll take a week or more to make the trip, too."

Sallie spoke up for the first time in several minutes. "That's why we need someone to help us, like an experienced guide and scout."

Fargo had been waiting for that. He had expected it more from McCabe than from Sallie, but there it was.

And for a second he couldn't help but consider it. After all, he was bound for Topeka, just like they were. It certainly wouldn't be out of his way if he rode along with them.

But it would take more than twice as long if he accompanied the wagons and had to match his pace to theirs. Henry Coleman's letter had made it sound like it was urgent that he see Fargo as soon as possible. Fargo had taken the man's money, so he felt a certain duty to fulfill that obligation before he took on any others.

"What about it, Mr. Fargo?" McCabe asked bluntly. "Do you think you can help us?"

"You do need a good experienced man to go with you the rest of the way," Fargo agreed as an idea came to him. "And I've got just the fella for you. His name is Reuben Sanborn."

2

"What?" Reuben exclaimed later that evening as Fargo explained the situation to him. "Me guide a bunch o' psalm-singin' do-gooders across the prairie to Topeka? Are you outta your mind, Skye?"

"They'll pay you," Fargo said, leaning on the bar in the Great Plains Palace.

A glint came into Reuben's eyes. "How much?"

"Fifty whole dollars."

"Fifty—" Reuben looked outraged for a second at the amount; then a thoughtful expression came over his rugged face. "In gold?"

Fargo nodded solemnly.

Reuben picked up the bucket of beer in front of him and drained it. He wiped the back of one big paw across his mouth. "Well, I reckon I could at least talk to 'em about it. I've always had a weakness for the pretty music gold coins make when they clink together."

Fargo laughed. "I thought you might say that. That's why I suggested you for the job."

"Tell me straight, though . . . they asked you first, didn't they?"

"They did," Fargo admitted. "But I've got to ride straight on to Topeka without delay. I can't take the time to stay with those wagons."

"Well," Reuben chuckled, "I reckon being second choice to the Trailsman ain't no cause for shame."

"You're a good man, Reuben. You'll do just as good a job for those folks as I could."

"Maybe. I'm a little worried about that McCabe fella tryin' to preach at me all the time, though. I ain't sayin' that I ain't religious, but I don't like to be yammered at."

Fargo knew what Reuben was talking about. Most men who spent their time surrounded by the magnificence of the frontier developed a feeling of kinship with the Creator. They had little patience, though, for the rituals of formal religion.

"McCabe's more interested in getting those supplies through than he is in proselytizing. I don't think he'll give you any trouble."

"And that daughter o' his . . . you say she's pretty?"

"Mighty pretty. But she packs iron, Reuben. I've got a feeling you'd do well to remember that."

"A gun-totin' female?" Reuben shook his shaggy head dolefully. "What's the world comin' to?"

"Just watch your step. I don't reckon Miss Sallie would take a gun to you unless you gave her a good reason."

"Don't you worry. I'll behave. I'd never live it down if a gal shot at me, let alone ventilated me!"

Fargo laughed. "Better get some sleep. Reverend McCabe wants to pull out first thing in the morning."

"Me workin' for a reverend . . . it just don't seem natural. Better'n sittin' around a town, though."

"That's what I thought. I'm not sure you're as ready to settle down as you claimed, Reuben."

The big mountain man grinned. "You're prob'ly right."

It was a stroke of luck that Reuben had been here

in the City of Kansas and had also been at loose ends. As soon as Fargo thought of him, he knew that Reuben was just the man the McCabes needed to help them get the supply train through to Topeka. Reuben was tough and experienced, and he was familiar with the trail. Fargo could push on now to his own appointment without worrying.

He had enjoyed the rest of his dinner with the McCabes, even though he could tell they were disappointed that he wasn't going to go along. He had promised that he would talk to Reuben, and he planned to be on hand the next morning when the wagons pulled out, just to make sure that Reuben showed up and that the arrangement would be satisfactory to all involved. Then he would ride out himself and head for Topeka.

Reuben had rented one of the rooms on the second floor of the Great Plains Palace. Fargo lingered in the saloon until his friend had gone up to turn in for the night. Then he left and walked toward the hotel where he was staying.

It was a cool, crisp autumn night. The air was clear, and as Fargo looked along the street he could see the lights of the little settlement of Wyandotte, across the river in Kansas Territory, glittering in the darkness. Wyandotte was one of the jumping-off places for immigrants headed west into the territory, but there weren't very many of those these days. Indeed, from the talk he had heard around town, the drought had reversed the normal course of travel. Folks were leaving Kansas now, abandoning their homesteads, instead of going west to make new lives for themselves.

The ones who held out and made it through these tough times would ultimately reap quite a reward, Fargo mused. The drought couldn't last forever, and once there was plenty of rain again, that would be some of the best farmland in the world over there.

The frontiersman in Fargo hated to see the prairie broken up by plows, hated to see mules and oxen plodding along where once swift Indian ponies had raced, but he was enough of a realist to know that it was inevitable. Folks had to eat, and someday the plains might be the breadbasket of the whole nation. Farms would cover the prairie from the Mississippi River to the Rocky Mountains.

He probably wouldn't live to see those days—they were still too far in the future—and that was all right, too, Fargo reflected.

The scuff of a boot somewhere close behind him broke into his thoughts. With alarm bells suddenly going off in his brain, he started to turn. A gun roared and muzzle flame stabbed at him from the darkness when he was only halfway around.

That move was enough to save his life. The slug sizzled past his body, missing him by mere inches. Fargo flung himself off the boardwalk and landed beside a water trough. Another shot blasted. The bullet kicked up dirt in the street as Fargo rolled behind the water trough. A third shot sounded, but the bushwhack lead couldn't penetrate the thick, pitch-lined wooden walls of the trough.

Fargo's Colt was in his hand by the time he came to a stop, lying on his belly. He hadn't even been aware of drawing the gun. But he knew what he was doing as he looped his thumb over the hammer, eared it back, and reared up just long enough to trigger a shot at the dark mouth of the alley where the would-be killer lurked. Instantly he dropped back down behind the protection of the water trough.

The thudding of footsteps to his left warned him. A second bushwhacker darted out of the shadows farther along the boardwalk, running out into the street so that he could get a shot at the Trailsman. Fargo rolled again, flattening out as much as possible as the second man fired. The slug whined over his head and smacked into the trough. Splinters stung Fargo's cheek.

Fargo fired twice at the shadowy figure to force him back toward the buildings. He knew he was vulnerable to attack again from the first man. Sure enough, another bullet from that direction kicked up dust right beside him.

The water trough didn't furnish enough cover to protect him from both angles when he was lying behind it, but it was the only bit of shelter within reach. Fargo did the only thing he could think of.

He surged up, rolled over the nearest side of the trough, and dropped into the water with a huge splash.

Now he had the walls of the trough between him and both bushwhackers. He held his Colt up, keeping it as dry as possible. He snapped another shot toward the alley and heard a man cry out in pain. Blind luck had guided his aim, Fargo knew, but he would take it. He gulped air into his lungs and ducked lower, putting his face under the surface of the water. More bullets thudded into the side of the trough, but none of them made it through.

By this time the sounds of the gun battle had reached all along the street, and men shouted questions as they hurried to see what was going on. Fargo thought the men who had ambushed him might take off instead of hanging around to be discovered. That would be a shame, because he sure would like to know who they were and why they had tried to kill him, but the way they had had him bracketed, a draw might be the best result he could hope for in this fight.

The echoes of the shots died away and no more reports sounded. Fargo was convinced the bushwhackers had lit a shuck. He was even more sure of it when an authoritative voice shouted, "You there in the water trough! Stand up, and keep your hands where I can see 'em!"

The law had arrived.

With the Colt raised above his head, Fargo used his other hand to lever himself to his feet. Water ran in streams from his soaked clothes. A chill went through him as the night air hit his wet skin.

Several figures approached him, and the one who had spoken before said, "We generally like to let our horses drink from those troughs, mister, instead of using them as swimming holes. What the hell's going on here?"

"Are you the marshal?" Fargo asked.

"That's right." The man came closer, so that Fargo could see he carried a shotgun. The faint glow from a window in a nearby building revealed a weather-beaten face under a black hat. A badge shone on his vest. "Marshal Ed Porter. Who're you?"

"Name's Skye Fargo. And I didn't jump in here because I wanted to take a midnight swim, Marshal. A couple of men just tried to kill me, and this was the best cover I could find."

Marshal Porter grunted in surprise. "Ambushed you, did they?"

Fargo nodded and pointed toward the alley. "One of them was lurking in there, the other one was farther along the boardwalk. They waited until I was between them and then opened up on me."

Porter turned his head and spoke to the men with him, probably his deputies. "All right, boys, looks like the ruckus is over. Go on back to making your rounds."

Fargo stepped out of the water trough, grimacing as his feet squelched in his boots. It would take a while for the boots and his buckskins to dry. Better that than having a few bullet holes in his hide, though.

"You got any idea why those fellas bushwhacked you, Fargo?" Porter went on. "Out to rob you, maybe?"

"Maybe," Fargo said. "I'm not carrying much money, though. If that's what they were after, they were wasting their time."

"Reckon they didn't know that. Or maybe they had some other reason for wanting you dead."

Fargo shook his head. "If they did, I can't think of what it might be."

He didn't think the gunmen had been robbers. A thief would have been more likely to hit him over the head. That was a lot quieter and would attract a lot less attention, so that the robber could go about his larcenous work in peace.

"Fargo," Marshal Porter mused. "I know that name. . . ."

Fargo was about to admit that he was the Trailsman, but before he could the lawman continued, "You're the fella who had that fight with Jed Brinker this afternoon."

"That's right," Fargo said.

"Brinker's a no-good son of a bitch, and his friends are more of the same. I'll bet it was him and one of his pards who ambushed you. Brinker wouldn't draw the line at back-shooting if he wanted to settle a score."

That possibility had already occurred to Fargo, and it seemed like the most likely explanation for the attempt on his life. He had played dumb about it, though, because he wanted to look into the matter himself. That wasn't going to be possible since the marshal had figured it out, too.

"You'd better watch your back, Fargo," Porter warned. "Were you hit? Need to see the doctor?"

Fargo shook his head. "They burned a lot of powder, but they missed all their shots. I'm not sure I did, though."

"You think you winged one of 'em?"

"I heard a yelp from the one in the alley. Why don't we take a look?"

Porter nodded. "Good idea. I've got some matches."

"So do I," Fargo said, "but I don't think they'll ever be any good again after that dunking."

He and Porter walked over to the mouth of the alley, and the marshal scraped a lucifer to life on the wall of one of the buildings. He held the flame down toward the ground while he and Fargo looked around. It took only a moment for Fargo to spot the small dark puddle in the dirt.

He touched it and held his finger in the light from the match. "Blood, all right. Not a lot, but enough to show that it wasn't just a crease."

"No, you tagged him pretty good," Porter agreed. "We have several doctors here in town. Tomorrow I'll check and see if any of them treated a bullet wound tonight. Chances are, though, whoever it was got one of his friends to pour some whiskey on it and wrap a bandage around it. Fellas like that generally patch up their own wounds."

Fargo nodded in agreement.

"And if it *was* Brinker and his bunch, they may not even be in town by tomorrow morning. They might ride out tonight."

"They're not from around here?" Fargo asked.

Porter dropped the match as it burned down close to his fingers. He ground it out with his boot heel and said, "Hardcases like that aren't from anywhere. They drift into a place, stay a while, and drift out again. They're always on the move because they're always up to no good. From what I've heard, though, Brinker and his friends spend most of their time over in the Kansas Territory, around Lawrence and Topeka."

So he might run into them again, Fargo thought. He didn't mind that idea at all. That impromptu bath in the water trough had been pretty unpleasant, and if Brinker had been the cause of it, then Fargo had a score of his own to settle now.

"Well, there's nothing that can be done about this tonight," Porter went on. "You'd better get out of those wet clothes, Fargo, before you catch your death of cold."

"I was thinking the same thing. I was on my way to the hotel anyway when they jumped me."

"I'll walk down there with you, just to make sure nobody tries anything else. Don't think they will, though."

Neither did Fargo, and as it turned out he and Porter were both right. A few minutes later he and the marshal reached the hotel. The clerk frowned as Fargo walked into the lobby dripping water, but he didn't say anything. The dark look on Fargo's face probably warned him not to.

"You got a place where these clothes can be hung up to dry?" Fargo asked.

The clerk nodded. "There's a clothesline out back, between the hotel and the barn."

"Can you send somebody up to my room to get them and hang them up after I take them off?"

"Sure. If you want, just put them in the hall outside your door. I'll have a boy pick them up and tend to them."

"Thanks," Fargo looked over in the corner of the

lobby, where a small fire glowed in a cast-iron stove. "I'm going to put my boots over there by the stove so they'll dry faster."

"Of course. If you need something else to wear, I might be able to get the owner of the emporium down the street to open for a little while, long enough to get some extra clothes sent up to you."

Fargo shook his head. "Thanks, but I've got a spare set of buckskins in my gear. The boots are a bigger problem."

Fargo pulled off his boots. He admired the clerk's restraint. The man had to be wondering how the hell he had gotten soaked like this.

"Come by my office in the morning," Marshal Porter told Fargo. "I'll let you know if anything has turned up, and you do likewise."

"Sure, Marshal." Porter left as Fargo placed his boots beside the stove.

He went back to the desk and asked the clerk, "You know Jed Brinker?"

"I know who he is, but I certainly wouldn't associate with the likes of him."

"If you see him skulking around here, let me know right away, will you?"

"Of course, Mr. Fargo." The clerk's frown deepened. "There's not going to be any gunplay here in the hotel, is there?"

"I hope not."

"Good. I heard the shooting down the street a while ago. It sounded like a war had broken out."

"Not a war," Fargo said. "Just an ambush."

He didn't add that he had been right in the middle of it. The clerk could draw that conclusion for himself.

Fargo went up to his room on the second floor and lit the lamp on the nightstand next to the bed with a dry match. He peeled off the wet duds, the buckskins making a soggy mess when they crumpled on the floor. Still wearing his long underwear, he opened the door and dropped the buckskins in the hallway. Then he closed the door, took off the underwear, and used a cloth to rub himself dry as best he could. Feeling considerably better, he pulled on the bottom half of a dry pair of long-handles.

A knock sounded on the door.

Fargo frowned. The clerk had said that one of the boys who worked in the hotel would collect the wet buckskins and hang them up to dry. He started toward the door, wondering what the problem was, when instinct prompted him to pluck his Colt from its holster where it lay with the coiled shell belt on the bed. Carrying the revolver, he went to the door and opened it.

The buckskins were gone, already picked up by the boy. Standing there instead was Sallie McCabe.

She arched her eyebrows at the sight of his bare chest covered with a thick mat of dark brown hair. "Mr. Fargo," she said coolly.

"Miss McCabe," he answered, equally coolly. If she expected him to jump and try to cover up, she was mistaken. "What are you doing here?"

"We heard there was some trouble after you left us this evening. You were involved in all that shooting a while ago?"

He nodded. "A couple of men bushwhacked me, tried to kill me. I figure it was that fella Brinker and one of his friends."

"You mean they tried to kill you just because you stepped in when Brinker picked a fight with one of our drivers?"

"It doesn't take much to set some men off," Fargo said. He smiled. "The important thing is that they missed."

"Yes, of course." Sallie looked down at the gun in his hand, which he now held beside his leg. "I suppose that's why you came to the door armed, just in case it was those men again."

Fargo said, "I'm in the habit of being careful. It's kept me alive this long."

Sallie's gaze was still lowered, but he could tell she wasn't looking at the Colt now. Her eyes had strayed to his crotch, where the underwear clearly outlined the thick length of his manhood and the heavy sacs underneath it. Her breath began to come a little faster, and a faint flush crept across her face.

"Was there anything else?" Fargo asked. He didn't mind Sallie getting herself a good look, but she was studying him like she intended to paint his portrait or something. A portrait without any clothes on.

She tore her gaze away and lifted it to his face again. Sounding a little confused, she said, "Oh . . . there was something else . . . oh, yes, did you talk to your friend about guiding our wagons to Topeka?"

"Yes, Reuben agreed to take the job. He'll be ready to leave first thing in the morning. I'll be there, too, to introduce him to you and your father."

"That's good. Thank you, Mr. Fargo."

When she still hesitated just outside his room, he put his free hand on the open door and asked again, "Was there anything else you wanted?"

Sallie took a deep breath and said, "Just this."

She stepped forward, put her arms around his neck, and came up on her toes as she pressed her mouth to his in a hot, urgent kiss.

Fargo wasn't surprised. He didn't pull away. Instead he slipped his left arm around her and pulled her even more tightly against him. Her breasts molded and flattened against his chest, and he felt her nipples hardening through the fabric of her dress.

When she broke the kiss she whispered, "I hope you don't think that was too bold of me."

"I like a bold woman who knows what she wants," Fargo told her.

She brought one hand down, slid it over his chest and belly, and then caressed his stiffening shaft through the long underwear. "Then you must like me," she said with a soft laugh, "because I certainly know what I want."

"Your father's a minister," Fargo pointed out.

"But before he took up preaching he was a freighter, and he cut a wide swath through all the ladies between here and Chicago. Some of them called him Bullwhip McCabe, but it wasn't because of that whip he carries."

Fargo couldn't help but raise an eyebrow and chuckle. "Really?"

"That's right. And I have the same appetite for pleasures of the flesh that he did when he was younger." Sallie bent her head forward and kissed his chest, then ran her tongue around one of his nipples. "I don't think it's the least bit sinful, either. Have you ever read the Song of Solomon?"

"I've glanced through it," Fargo said.

"It talks about how beautiful it is for a man and a woman to lie together, and that's right there in the Bible."

Fargo wasn't going to stand around arguing theology with her. "And we're right here practically in the hall."

"We can fix that," Sallie said. She gave him a little push and shut the door behind her as she came into the room.

She wouldn't have been able to budge Fargo if he didn't want her to. Now that they were alone, he set the Colt aside and drew her into his arms again for a proper kiss. She was here of her own free will, and she was more than old enough to know what she was doing. He was pretty sure she had done it before, too.

The dress she wore buttoned up the back. Deftly he began to unfasten the buttons. He pulled the dress down over her shoulders, pushed it over her hips, and let it fall around her feet. The silky undergarments she wore came off just as easily. When her breasts were bared he saw that they were large and firm, pale globes of flesh crowned with dark brown nipples the size of silver dollars. He took first one and then the other into his mouth, sucking and licking. Sallie gave a little whimper of pleasure.

She tugged at his long underwear and managed to get them down over his hips, freeing his stiff organ. Wrapping her hands around it, she sighed. "So big," she said, "and it's going to feel so good inside me."

Fargo pushed the gun belt aside on the bed and stretched out on top of the covers. It was cool in the room, but both of them were so overheated with passion that they didn't notice. Sallie climbed on top of him, swinging around so that she faced away from him. She leaned forward, steadied his pole with both hands, and began kissing and licking it.

That put her in perfect position for Fargo to reach the wet, heated opening between her legs. He used his thumbs to spread the fleshy folds apart and then delved between them with his tongue. Sallie caught her breath and began to pump her hips a little, working her femininity back and forth on Fargo's lips and tongue.

After a moment she remembered what she had started doing to him and resumed the exquisite torture. She closed her lips around the head of his shaft and began to suck, gradually working her way down until more and more of the thick pole of male flesh was buried in the hot, wet cavern of her mouth. Fargo restrained the urge to thrust down her throat. He didn't want to gag her.

For long minutes they pleasured each other that way. Sallie finally lifted her head, releasing his member, and swung around again. This time she poised her hips above his and guided his shaft into her as she sank down on it. He didn't encounter any resistance, confirming his suspicion that she had been with men before. He wasn't necessarily opposed to deflowering virgins—he had done it before, under the right circumstances—but he was able to throw himself into the lovemaking with a little more enthusiasm when his partner had some experience.

Sallie seemed to have had plenty, judging by the easy way she began riding him. Her hips rose and fell smoothly as she lifted herself nearly off of him, then came down again to take the entire length of him inside her. She gasped in excitement every time she bottomed out.

Fargo grasped her hips and added his own thrusts to the mixture. She was beautiful, he thought as he looked up, her heavy breasts swaying in front of his face. She smiled down at him. Their pace increased as she whispered, "Deeper, Skye, deeper."

His climax burst on him almost unexpectedly, shaking him with its power. He emptied himself inside her in spurt after white-hot spurt, and at the same time spasms of culmination rippled through her. Fargo's hips jerked a couple of final times as her inner muscles milked him of the last he had to give her.

Then she lay down on his chest and breathed hard, trying to recover from the depth of her climax. Fargo felt pretty much the same way. After a moment he regained enough strength to stroke her flanks as his shaft gradually softened inside her.

"I think I'm glad you're not going with us to Topeka," she whispered.

"Why?" Fargo asked.

"Because I'd want to be doing that with you all the time, and I think it might just kill me!"

Fargo laughed softly.

She propped herself up on an elbow and said, "It's not funny. You're a dangerous man, Skye Fargo. You could love a girl to death."

"I never have before," he told her.

She reached down to where he had slipped out of her and began massaging him. His manhood started to harden again almost instantly.

"I don't mind living dangerously," she said with a smile.

3

The hour was late when Sallie slipped out of Fargo's hotel room to return to the camp where her father and the rest of the men taking supplies to Kansas Territory were staying. Fargo felt well rested, though, when he got up before dawn the next morning, pulled on the clean pair of buckskins, and went downstairs for breakfast.

He picked up his boots as he went through the lobby. A night of sitting beside the heat of the stove had dried them for the most part. They were still a little damp in places, but Fargo could wear them that way.

With a good meal and a pot of coffee in him, he left the hotel and walked along the street toward the wagons. The eastern sky glowed a bright orange, but the sun hadn't yet peeked over the horizon. Fargo's breath fogged in front of his face in the chilly air.

He spotted Reuben Sanborn talking to Joshua McCabe beside the lead wagon. Reuben held the reins of his horse, a big black gelding. As Fargo walked along the line of wagons toward them he looked for Sallie, but he didn't see her.

Reuben and McCabe were a good match, both of them burly, powerful men, one dark and one fair. McCabe was considerably older, too, although he still had plenty of vitality. They turned to greet Fargo as he walked up to them.

"Good morning, Skye," Reuben boomed.

"Hello, Mr. Fargo," McCabe said.

Fargo nodded to them. "I came down here to introduce you fellas to each other, but I see you've already met."

"Yes, we're getting along just fine," McCabe said. "Mr. Sanborn seems like the perfect choice to help us get to Topeka safely."

"I told you, make it Reuben," the big mountain man said. "I may not be the trailsman that Skye here is, but I can find my way, don't worry about that."

Fargo smiled. "Reuben's being too modest. He's been to see the elephant. You can count on that." Fargo looked along the line of wagons, noting with satisfaction the way the teams were hitched up and the vehicles cared for. "Looks like you've done a good job. When are you pulling out?"

"Any time now," McCabe answered. "To tell you the truth, we're just waiting for Sallie . . . and here she comes now, it looks like."

Fargo turned and saw Sallie hurrying toward the front of the wagon train. She was back in the trail clothes she had worn the day before, including the holstered six-gun on her hip. She smiled as she came up to Fargo, Reuben, and McCabe.

"Good morning," McCabe greeted her. "How'd you sleep?"

Sallie glanced at Fargo and then said, "Just fine. Very restful."

If McCabe noticed anything odd about the way she answered, he didn't show it. He just rubbed his hands together and said, "Good. We're ready to get started, then."

Fargo spoke up. "Sallie, this is the man I told you about, Reuben Sanborn."

"Hello, Mr. Sanborn," she said with a smile.

The big mountain man jerked his floppy-brimmed hat off his head. "Ma'am," he said politely. "I'm mighty honored to make your acquaintance."

Fargo could see that Sallie was pleased by Reuben's rough gallantry. He didn't expect any sort of romance to develop between the two of them during the trip to Topeka, but stranger things had happened. If he was still in town when the wagon train got there, he would look them up and see how things were going.

"Well, I won't keep you," he said. He shook hands with McCabe and Reuben. "I know you're anxious to get started. Good luck on the trip."

"Will we see you anywhere along the way?" Sallie asked quickly.

"Maybe, but I'll just be riding past," Fargo told her. "I have to get on to Topeka as soon as I can."

"Good luck to you, too, Mr. Fargo," McCabe said. He waved Sallie toward the second wagon in line. "Let's go."

Reuben swung up on his horse and said, "So long, Skye."

"Take care, old hoss," Fargo said with a grin. "And keep your eyes open. That's mighty precious cargo you're guarding."

Reuben glanced toward Sallie. "I know."

Fargo tried not to grin too much as he turned away. Reuben was obviously smitten with the honey-haired young woman—and Fargo didn't blame him a bit for feeling that way.

He walked along the wagons, and as he passed the one where Sallie had climbed to the driver's box, she stopped him by holding a hand down to him.

"Good-bye, Skye," she said quietly as he clasped her hand. "I'm going to miss you."

"I'll miss you, too," Fargo replied honestly. He liked Sallie McCabe; there was no denying that. But he was a long way from liking her enough to even consider giving up his footloose ways. Not that she had asked him to, he reminded himself. There was nothing clinging about her attitude.

"I hope we run into each other again sometime."

"That would be nice," Fargo agreed. She let go of his hand and he stepped back to watch while the wagon train full of supplies got under way. Reuben went first, of course, riding ahead of the lead wagon. One by one the drivers got their teams moving, and soon the whole line of wagons was rolling west toward the ferry that crossed the Missouri River.

Fargo didn't wait until they were out of sight. He turned back toward the hotel. It wouldn't take him long to gather his gear and saddle up the Ovaro. He had to stop by the marshal's office, too, and see if Porter had discovered anything about the men who had bushwhacked Fargo the previous night.

Porter hadn't, but again he warned Fargo to be careful. "If Brinker was responsible for what happened, he's liable to try again."

"I'm used to keeping my eyes open," Fargo assured the lawman.

Less than half an hour after the wagons left the City of Kansas, so did Fargo, riding out of town and heading west.

The trail ran along the south side of the Kansas River. The wheels of the wagon train had left ruts in the dust, as had numerous wagon trains before it. The landscape was flat, broken only by occasional stretches of gentle undulations that weren't tall enough to be called hills or even rises. The ground was covered with a thick carpet of bluestem, and stands of cottonwood trees—their limbs bare now because of the season— grew here and there, especially along the numerous small streams and creeks that flowed into the river.

It was pretty country, Fargo thought, not spectacularly beautiful like the mountains farther west but still pleasing to the eye. Of course, he was the sort of man who could find something to like about almost anywhere he found himself, as long as it wasn't too crowded with people.

That certainly wasn't the case here. Over the past decade there had been a considerable amount of folks settling in Kansas Territory, but the homesteads were large and spread far apart. He passed only occasional low-lying sod cabins, and many of them appeared to be deserted, as were most of the cultivated fields he passed. Some settlers close to the river had been able to haul water from the stream to irrigate their fields, but the drought had been so fierce that even that hadn't been enough in many places. The river itself was low, filling only a part of its bed.

The drought had to break sometime, Fargo told himself. Like all men who spent most of their lives outdoors, he knew something about the weather. He had seen dry spells before, and the one thing they had in common was that sooner or later they all came to an end.

That couldn't come soon enough for the settlers here in Kansas Territory.

Maybe the supplies being taken to Topeka by the wagon train would help people get through the worst of it. Food, tools, seed for next year's crop—all of it had been donated by caring people across the Midwest, and it would be distributed free of charge to the homesteaders. Fargo couldn't help but admire the way his fellow Americans had pitched in to help those less fortunate.

He saw the dust rising ahead, stirred up by the slow-moving wagon train. A few miles later he came in sight of the lumbering vehicles. He swung to the left and rode past them, waving to the drivers as he went by. Sallie gave him a particularly enthusiastic wave. Fargo returned it, but he didn't rein in to talk to her, even though a part of him wanted to. He had made his decision to push on to Topeka as quickly as he could, and he wasn't going back on that.

However, he did pause for a moment to speak to Reuben when he came alongside the mountain man, a couple of hundred yards in front of the lead wagon.

"Any trouble yet?" Fargo asked.

Reuben shook his head. "Nope. We only just left the settlements, though. I ain't seen hide nor hair of anybody who might bother us."

"Maybe it'll stay like that all the way to Topeka," Fargo said. "There's no Indian trouble in this part of the territory, so at least you don't have to worry about that."

"I ain't worried about much of anything," Reuben said confidently. "We'll be fine."

Fargo lifted a hand in farewell, and rode on. Even though he was holding the Ovaro to an easy pace, he still pulled away quickly from the much slower wagons. They fell behind him and then dropped out of sight.

It was midmorning when Fargo spotted some dust on the other side of the river. From the looks of it, a good-sized group of riders was heading west over there, and moving along pretty quickly. Fargo frowned slightly. Why would anyone be moving at that pace all the way out here?

He remembered what Marshal Porter had told him

about Brinker and his bunch drifting around between Lawrence and Topeka. Fargo wondered if they could be the riders north of the river.

He wasn't going to waste a lot of time worrying about it. If trouble came, he would deal with it.

At midday he stopped on the bank of a little creek to eat some jerky from his saddlebags and a couple of biscuits he had brought from the hotel dining room. He had more biscuits cached for his supper that night. The stallion grazed on the bluestem, and both he and Fargo drank their fill from the stream. Satisfied and rested, Fargo pushed on.

The dust on the other side of the river had disappeared. Fargo hadn't seen the riders stop.

It was the middle of the afternoon when Fargo suddenly heard whoops and gunshots ahead of him on the trail. He stiffened in the saddle for a second, then heeled the Ovaro into a run. He had no idea what sort of ruckus he was galloping toward, but he wasn't the sort of man who could sit back and ignore the plight of someone who was in trouble.

Leaning forward in the saddle he raced along until he came in sight of a wagon that was being driven with reckless abandon over the rutted trail. A gang of men on horseback rode alongside, yelling at the driver and firing pistols over his head. There were bullet holes in the high wooden sides that enclosed the back of the vehicle. He urged the stallion on to greater speeds, and as he closed the gap, he pulled his Henry rifle from its saddle scabbard.

Nobody could fire with great accuracy from the hurricane deck of a racing horse, but Fargo was as good a shot under those conditions as anybody. As he guided the Ovaro with his knees he drew a bead on one of the riders and squeezed off a shot. The bullet just missed, whining past the man's ear. He jerked his head around to look back at Fargo with astonishment, and yelled out to the others.

Two riders wheeled their horses around to face their attacker. Smoke and flame spouted from their gun muzzles as they galloped toward the Trailsman.

Fargo levered another round into the Henry's chamber and fired again. The lead rider dropped his gun, clutched at his shoulder, and almost fell from his horse. His mount slowed to a stop as he sagged in the saddle.

Slugs from the other man's gun kicked up dust in the trail in front of Fargo. Coolly, the Trailsman fired twice more, and with his second shot the other man flipped backward, driven out of the saddle by the bullet that had caught him in the heart. One foot hung in the stirrup as his horse dragged his limp corpse about twenty yards before the animal came to a stop.

The wounded man turned his horse and fled after his companions, shouting a weak warning. They looked back and saw Fargo closing in, with one of their own dead in the dust and another covered in blood.

A bullet ripped off the wagon driver's tall beaver hat. He dropped the reins and slid forward on the seat, slumping on the floorboards of the driver's box.

Fargo bit back a curse. The driver was either dead or unconscious, and the big horses in his team were still running full out, stampeding now with no hand on the reins.

Fargo snapped a couple more shots at the gunmen. They veered away from the wagon and galloped off across country. Fargo had the choice of going after them or trying to stop the runaway wagon.

That wasn't really a choice as far as Fargo was concerned. The man on the wagon might still be alive, and Fargo had to help him if he could.

He slid the Henry back into its sheath and spurred on the Ovaro. The stallion responded gallantly, surging forward like a streak of lightning. The horses in the wagon team were big, strong animals, but they were no match for the Ovaro's blistering speed. Fargo began to catch up, and a few moments later he drew alongside the careening wagon.

Even under these desperate circumstances, his brain took note of the writing and the picture painted on the side of the wagon. A bank of dark clouds hung over a green, fertile landscape. Rain fell from those clouds, watering the crops below. Arching above, in garish red letters, were the words PROFESSOR GIDEON SPAULDING—CLOUD WIZARD AND RAINMAKER EXTRAORDINAIRE!

A rainmaker was just what Kansas Territory needed right now, Fargo thought, although he had never seen one who hadn't turned out to be a charlatan.

Fargo brought the stallion closer to the wagon. He grabbed a brass bar that was bolted to the side and kicked his feet from the stirrups. He leaned over farther and grasped the bar with his other hand as he slipped out of the saddle.

He hung there for a few seconds with his feet dangling just inches above the ground racing past underneath, before he was able to pull himself up. He got a toehold with one foot, shifted a hand to get a better grip, and hauled himself onto the box.

Fargo snatched up the fallen reins and pulled back, bracing his feet against the floorboards. Gradually the team slowed and came to a stop. He wrapped the reins around the brake lever and turned his attention to the man at his feet.

As Fargo bent over the man let out a groan. One side of his face was covered with blood. Carefully, Fargo turned his head and saw the crimson streak in the man's silvery hair, just above the left ear. A bullet had grazed his skull and knocked him out, but that was the extent of his injuries. The wound looked much worse than it actually was.

Carefully, Fargo lifted the man from the wagon and stretched him out on the ground. He was short and thickset, weighing quite a bit.

Fargo unlatched the back door of the wagon and peered inside. The wagon was filled with all sorts of odd-looking trinkets, but Fargo was able to find a blanket and some rags. He folded the blanket and slipped it under the unconscious man's head. He used water from his canteen to wet a rag and cleaned away the blood from around the wound.

The man's eyelids fluttered open. He struggled to say something, but Fargo stopped him. "Just take it easy, mister. You're all right."

The man subsided and managed a tiny nod. He closed his eyes as Fargo continued working on him. At the same time Fargo remained alert just in case those gun-throwers doubled back.

When Fargo was finished, the wounded man still looked pretty gory with blood smeared on his face, but the gash on his head had stopped bleeding. The man opened his eyes and said, "Am . . . am I going to die?"

"Not from that scratch on your noggin," Fargo said. "But I expect you'll have a blue devil of a headache tomorrow morning."

The man sighed. "Those bastards must have seen the blood and thought they'd blown my brains out. They would have killed me if you hadn't come along when you did."

"Why in blazes would they want to do that? Did you know them?"

"Never saw them before," the man muttered. "Ruffians like that don't need much of an excuse to go after someone, though."

"That's true. Are you Professor Spaulding?"

The man's eyes cut toward the brightly painted wagon. "Indeed I am. And you are? . . ."

"Skye Fargo."

"Well, I certainly thank you, Mr. Fargo. I suspect I owe you my life."

"You're welcome. And if you can really make it rain in Kansas, Professor, then I'll have done a double good deed."

"If?" Spaulding pushed himself up on an elbow and winced as the movement made his head hurt. Clearly, though, he was determined to defend his honor. "I'll have you know, my friend, that I've brought blessed moisture to a thirsty land many times in my long career. You are looking at none other than the world's leading expert in the science of rainmaking."

Fargo tried not to grin. "Well, I hope you're successful here, Professor. This territory's been mighty dry for a long time."

"Yes, I know. That's why the citizens of Topeka sent for me. My experiments are to be the highlight of the Shawnee County Fair."

This was the first time Fargo had heard anything about a county fair. Considering the dire circumstances in which the settlers hereabouts found themselves, he wouldn't have figured that they had anything to celebrate. On the other hand, maybe when things were bad was the best time for folks to get together and try to enjoy themselves for a little while. A celebration might be just what they needed to help them get through this rough patch.

He helped Professor Spaulding to his feet. "If you've got any whiskey, we ought to clean that bullet crease and then bandage it," Fargo suggested.

"As it just so happens, I, ah, do have a bottle in the

wagon. For medicinal purposes only, of course, but I think this certainly qualifies. If you'll kindly give me an arm on which to steady myself, I'll have a look. . . ."

After rummaging around in the back of the wagon for a few moments, Spaulding brought out a brown glass bottle with a peeling label. "Ah!" he said as he uncorked it. He lifted the bottle to his mouth and took a long swallow.

"Better leave some for cleaning that wound," Fargo advised dryly.

"Of course, of course." Spaulding handed over the bottle.

Fargo found another rag, poured whiskey on it, and said to the professor, "This is going to hurt."

Spaulding waved a pudgy hand. "Proceed with your ministrations, my friend."

He winced and muttered curses as Fargo cleaned the wound with the whiskey-soaked rag. When Fargo was done, Spaulding said, "I believe I have a clean shirt in here, as well, that you can use for a bandage, my young frontier Lochinvar."

Fargo chuckled. "I'm no knight in shining armor, Professor."

"You've read Sir Walter Scott?" Spaulding sounded surprised.

"He's a mite long-winded, but he spins a good yarn." Fargo took the clean shirt from Spaulding, cut a strip off the tail with his Arkansas Toothpick, and tied it carefully around the professor's head so that the wound was protected.

"My thanks, sir." Spaulding looked around. "Where's my hat?"

"It flew off when one of those fellas nicked you." Fargo jerked a thumb over his shoulder. "It should be back up the road a piece. I'll go take a look."

He whistled and the Ovaro came trotting over to him. The stallion had been grazing on a patch of grass nearby.

"What a magnificent animal!" Spaulding stared at the big black-and-white horse with open admiration.

Fargo swung up into the saddle and reached down to pat the stallion on the shoulder. "We've been down a lot of trails together, this old fella and me. Be back in a minute."

He rode along the trail until he spotted the professor's hat lying on the ground. It had a chunk missing out of the crown, Fargo saw when he picked it up. The professor really had dodged death by a narrow margin.

Not far away lay the body of the man Fargo had killed in the brief gunfight, abandoned by his companions. Fargo rode over and looked down at him for a long moment, studying the beard-stubbled, coarse features. The man was a typical hardcase in worn and patched range clothes. Fargo couldn't recall ever seeing him before.

Spaulding fumed when he saw the hole in his hat. "The bounders!" he exclaimed. "There's not another beaver hat of that quality between here and St. Louis. Trying to kill a man is bad enough, but to shoot a hole in a perfectly good hat . . . that's unforgivable!"

Fargo laughed and shook his head. He looked over the wagon and the team and said, "This is a mighty fancy outfit you've got, Professor."

"Only the best," Spaulding said. The horses wore silver-studded harnesses and had purple plumes strapped onto their heads. "People expect it."

Fargo leaned forward in the saddle and grinned. "You wouldn't happen to have sold a little snake oil in your time, would you, Professor?"

That brought the sort of indignant, sputtering reaction that Fargo expected. "Young man, if you hadn't come to my assistance earlier, I'd be forced to thrash you for that insinuation! Consider yourself fortunate that I'm in your debt."

"I'll do that. Reckon you're up to handling your team again?"

"Of course." Spaulding started to climb onto the wagon. He was halfway up when he suddenly let out a moan and started to fall backward.

Fargo leaned over from the saddle and reached out quickly to grab the older man's arm. He steadied Spaulding until the professor was able to climb onto the box.

"Again you were there when I needed you, Mr. Fargo," Spaulding said. "An unexpected wave of dizziness struck me."

"That comes from getting clipped on the head by a bullet," Fargo told him. He glanced at the sky. It was late enough in the afternoon now so that only an hour or two of daylight remained. "I'll ride along and make camp with you tonight."

Spaulding looked grateful. "I hesitated to ask, but I hoped you might be amenable to the idea of the two of us traveling together. That is, if you're on your way to Topeka, too."

"I am," Fargo said as the professor got the team moving. He rode alongside the wagon. "I'm in a bit of a hurry, though, so we may not be able to stick together all the way. I sort of want to make sure you're all right before I move on."

"The Chinese say that if you save a man's life, you're then bound to him forever. Interesting people, the Chinese. Terrible heathens, of course, but still interesting."

Fargo didn't intend to take care of Spaulding from now on just because he had given the professor a hand in that ruckus. But he supposed one night wouldn't delay him too much.

They made camp in a patch of cottonwoods along a creek. Fargo built a fire and heated up some beans that the professor had in the wagon, adding his bag of biscuits to the meal. Even though Spaulding had the fancy wagon and the fine team of horses, there was an air of genteel poverty about the man. Fargo suspected Spaulding wasn't as well off as he pretended to be.

After they had eaten, Fargo put out the campfire. No point in announcing their presence to anybody who happened to be riding across the prairie, he thought. Spaulding brought out a couple of cigars and offered Fargo one.

"Don't mind if I do," the Trailsman said. He and Spaulding lit up, and they sat there on the trunk of a fallen cottonwood, smoking contentedly.

Fargo's mood of contentment vanished abruptly, however, when he heard a series of faint popping sounds. He came to his feet.

"What's wrong?" Spaulding asked.

"Didn't you hear that?"

"I'm afraid not. What was it?"

"Gunfire," Fargo replied grimly. He stared into the darkness to the east, the direction the shots had come from, and after a moment his keen eyes picked up an orange glow close to the horizon. Something was on fire back there.

And the only thing Fargo could think of that was big enough to give off that much light as it burned was the McCabe wagon train.

4

Fargo had hobbled the horses from the professor's team but had left the Ovaro loose as he always did, knowing that the big stallion wouldn't drift too far from camp. He let out a shrill whistle to summon the horse and snatched up blanket and saddle.

Getting the Ovaro ready to ride was the work of mere moments. As Fargo tightened the last cinch, Spaulding asked, "Where are you going?"

"I've got some friends a few miles back with a wagon train," Fargo explained as he picked up his hat and put it on. "I think they might be in trouble."

"I could accompany you—" Spaulding began.

"Appreciate the offer, Professor, but there's no time. If I'm not back by morning, push on without me!"

Fargo swung up into the saddle and heeled the stallion into a run.

He had worried that the cargo of supplies would be too tempting a target for desperadoes to pass up, but he hadn't expected the wagon train to be hit on the first night out. He had thought the danger would be worse when they were farther west.

Obviously that wasn't the case, because the shooting continued as Fargo galloped on through the night. He pulled up from time to time to listen, and each time he did he heard the ominous popping in the distance.

The fire must not have been too bad, though, because the orange glow in the sky died down. It didn't make sense that thieves would set fire to the wagons, Fargo thought. They would want to steal what was inside those vehicles, not destroy the cargo. However, it was conceivable that one or two of the wagons might have been set ablaze accidentally during the attack.

Fargo didn't know how far ahead of the wagon train he had been when he camped with the professor. Sounds could travel quite a distance over this flat prairie in the cold, clear night air. He had no trouble following the road in the moonlight, and he estimated he had gone several miles when he caught sight of several small fires up ahead and knew they must mark the site of the wagon train camp.

What looked like fireflies winked in the darkness surrounding the camp, but Fargo knew those flashes of light didn't come from harmless insects. They were the muzzle flashes of guns as night riders attacked the wagon train.

Fargo pulled the Henry from its sheath as he galloped closer. Suddenly, a rider veered toward him out of the darkness and motioned for him to rein in. The man held a revolver in his hand, and a spray of silvery moonlight revealed a bandanna across his face. He called in a muffled voice, "Damn, they're puttin' up a hell of a fight!" Suddenly he realized that Fargo wasn't wearing a mask. "You're not one of us!"

The gun in his hand jerked toward Fargo.

"That's right, I'm not," Fargo grated as he fired the Henry before the outlaw could bring the gun to bear. The man grunted in pain and dropped his weapon, slumping forward in the saddle as his horse began to dance around nervously. The horse bolted. The wounded outlaw fell off and sprawled limply on the ground, either dead or hurt badly enough that he was out of the fight.

But he was just one of many, Fargo thought. He judged by the guns flashing around him that at least a dozen men were attacking the wagons, and probably more.

A bullet whined past his head. He thought the shot came from the circle of wagons beside the river. It was just a wild shot, fired blindly by one of the defenders, but one of those could kill a man just as dead as any other kind.

Reuben had formed the wagons into a tight circle placed close beside the river, not only so that the water would be handy but also because the stream furnished some protection from that side. The desperadoes couldn't attack Indian-style, riding around and around the wagons as they poured lead into the circle. They had to come at the wagons from three sides instead of four.

Figuring that he could do more good out here than he could if he joined the defenders inside the circle, Fargo slipped down from the saddle and sent the Ovaro trotting back out of danger with a slap on his rump. He worked his way behind the attackers.

The shots gave away their positions. Fargo snuck up behind a man crouched in some brush, blazing away at the wagons with a rifle. Moving silently, Fargo stepped in and smashed the butt of his Henry against the man's head. The outlaw went down like a puppet with its strings cut, out cold. He took the man's rifle and pistol, unloaded them, and threw them off in the brush as far as he could. Then he cat-footed on, looking for another of the outlaws.

He knocked out two more of the raiders, then stiffened as somewhere nearby a man bellowed, "Light the torches! If we can't take 'em, we'll burn 'em out, damn it!"

Fargo bit back a curse as he realized he no longer had time for stealth. He stood up straight, brought the rifle to his shoulder, and cranked off four shots as fast as he could in the direction of the voice. From the corner of his eye he saw a spurt of flame and turned as a man with a blazing torch drew back his arm to throw it toward the wagons. Instantly, Fargo snapped the rifle to his shoulder and fired. The torch-wielder spun off his feet and dropped the burning brand beside him. The dry bluestem ignited with a *whoosh*!

The flames spread rapidly, and by their light Fargo picked out several more of the masked outlaws. He sent bullets whistling around their heads. Somebody yelled, "Let's get outta here!"

That was all it took to break the back of the attack. Outlaws forgot about the wagons and ran for their horses. Fargo let them go. He doubled back to the men he had knocked out and disarmed and found that they were gone. They must have come to and fled with their companions.

Fargo didn't relax. Although some of the raiders had taken off, others could still be lurking around. He was wary as he whistled for the Ovaro.

No one took any potshots at him as he mounted up and rode toward the wagons. The grass fire was already dying out, the flames having been blown by the light breeze against the rutted, dusty trail where there was nothing to burn. If the wind had been from another direction the fire would have spread much farther and been a disaster.

As Fargo rode toward the wagons, he thought about the voice he had heard shouting orders. Something about it was familiar, even though it had been muffled by the man's mask, but he couldn't place it. A moment later another voice shouted, this one from inside the circle of wagons. "Who's out there?" it demanded. "Stop or I'll shoot!"

Fargo recognized this voice as belonging to Joshua McCabe. He called back, "It's Skye Fargo! Hold your fire!"

"Mr. Fargo!" McCabe exclaimed. "Come on in!"

As Fargo rode up to the wagons he saw that one of them had indeed burned. But losing one wagon and its contents was a heap better than having the outlaws loot the whole train, he thought. He guided the Ovaro through the narrow gap between two of the wagons and was greeted by several men, including McCabe.

Fargo didn't see Sallie or Reuben Sanborn, and that realization made a chill go through him.

He dismounted and said to McCabe, "What happened?"

"They came out of nowhere, like wild Indians!" the wagon master said. "Reuben posted guards, but they didn't warn us. I think something must have happened to them."

Probably the outlaws had snuck up on the sentries and cut their throats, Fargo thought grimly. They would be able to tell when they took a look around in the morning.

McCabe went on. "Then before we knew what was happening, they were shooting at us. They wounded a couple of men, and one of the bullets broke a lantern that set one of the wagons on fire."

"Where's Reuben?" he asked.

McCabe looked worried. "He was one of the men who got hit right away. We pulled him under one of the wagons. I don't know how he is, but Sallie is with him."

"She's all right?" Fargo asked quickly.

"As far as I know."

Fargo was relieved to hear that, but he was worried about Reuben. He had gotten his friend into this in the first place. With McCabe leading the way, Fargo hurried across the circle toward the wagon where the wounded Reuben Sanborn had been taken.

Fargo knelt beside the wagon and looked underneath. From the light of the campfires he saw Reuben lying there, a crude, bloody bandage wrapped around his right shoulder. Sallie sat beside him, pillowing his head on her lap. She didn't seem to mind that his blood was staining her skirt.

"Skye!" she exclaimed when she saw Fargo. "I thought I heard your voice, but I decided I must be dreaming."

Fargo summoned up a smile. "It's me, all right," he said. "How's Reuben?"

The big mountain man's eyes opened, and he rumbled, "I hurt like hell, thank you very much! I reckon my collarbone's probably busted."

"I'm sorry to hear that," Fargo told him with a grin. "But I'm mighty glad to see that you're still alive, you old grizzly."

"I'm alive, all right, but no damned good to anybody like this."

"Hush," Sallie told him. "You shouldn't talk like that, Reuben. It's not your fault."

"The hell it's not. You folks trusted me to get these wagons through, and I've fouled it all up the first night on the trail!"

"Sallie's right, Reuben," Fargo said. "This ambush isn't your fault. In fact, if you hadn't set up camp the way you did, those raiders might have overrun you and taken the wagons without any trouble."

In a surly, pained voice, Reuben said, "Yeah, maybe. But what are we going to do now? We're shorthanded, and I won't be in any shape to do any scouting for a long time."

"Don't worry about that," Fargo said without hesitation. "I'll take over that chore."

Sallie said, "I thought you had an appointment you had to get to in Topeka."

"It can wait." Fargo still planned to talk to Henry Coleman, but the meeting would just have to be postponed until the supply train reached Topeka. Under the circumstances, he couldn't abandon them. It was too likely that those desperadoes would return and make another try for the supplies.

"Thanks, Skye," Reuben said. "I'm sorry you've got to pull my fat out of the fire."

"Don't worry about that," Fargo assured him. "There's nothing in Topeka that can't wait a few days."

He hoped that turned out to be true.

The rest of the night passed quietly. In the morning Fargo rode out to make sure that none of the wounded outlaws had been left behind. He found some dark splashes on the ground where blood had been spilled, but no bodies. Either he hadn't killed any of them, or their friends had carried the bodies away.

Unfortunately the three guards were all dead, just as Fargo feared they would be. He found their bodies sprawled in the brush the night before, after the attack. This morning Joshua McCabe was putting together a burial detail.

"We'll see that they're laid to rest properly and decently," McCabe declared.

Of the wounded men with the wagon train, Reuben's injury was the worst. The others just had bullet creases, painful but not incapacitating. When the graves were ready, everyone gathered for the brief funeral service. Reuben had to lean on Fargo's shoulder for support. Sallie stood on Reuben's other side and held his arm to steady him.

McCabe spoke the words over the graves, his voice rolling out over the prairie as he commended the souls of those who were lost into the hands of the Lord. Half the sky was covered with clouds, and as McCabe prayed the wind blew those clouds so that shifting patterns of sunlight and shadow played over the land, the mourners, and the mounds of raw earth that marked the fresh graves. Fargo hadn't known the men who had died, but even he felt the emotion of the moment.

The time for grieving had to be short. Soon the wagons were rolling again. There had been a few extra men along on the trip to help with loading and unloading the cargo. Now they were pressed into service as drivers, and there were just enough to go around. If anyone else couldn't handle a team for any reason, Fargo would have to take it. He didn't want to do that because he was more valuable to the party on horseback, scouting ahead and watching for any signs of trouble.

With luck it wouldn't come to that, he told himself as he trotted the Ovaro alongside the line of wagons. A bed had been made in one for Reuben, and Fargo lifted his hand in a wave as he rode past.

Pulling the stallion back to a walk beside McCabe's vehicle, Fargo said to the wagon master, "I'll be a couple of hundred yards ahead most of the time. If I range out farther than that I'll still try to stay in sight. Fire a shot if you need me."

"Do you think those men will come back, Mr. Fargo?" McCabe asked.

"There's no telling," Fargo said with a shake of his head. "If they want those supplies badly enough, they might. On the other hand we may have hurt them enough so that they're all off licking their wounds somewhere."

"I'll pray that's the case."

Fargo lifted a hand in farewell and let the Ovaro stretch his legs. He didn't slow the stallion to a walk again until he was well ahead of the wagons.

Fargo wondered how Professor Spaulding was faring. It was unlikely that the supply train would catch up with the rainmaker. Spaulding couldn't travel very fast, either, but if he had moved on this morning as Fargo had suggested, he would have a lead on the wagon train and probably wouldn't lose it.

The landscape had a parched look to it. The grass, while still thick, was dry and made a rustling sound as it waved in the breeze. The ground was hard and honeycombed with wide cracks.

In a month or so, the first of the winter storms would come roaring down out of Canada. In a normal year, heavy snow would fall, and when the snow melted it would provide moisture to the thirsty land.

But it might not be enough. The previous winter had been mild, and it took quite a bit of snow to amount to very much water in the spring. That was no substitute for a good soaking rain. The way things were, though, Kansas Territory would take what it could get.

At midday Fargo rode back to the wagons and ate with McCabe, Sallie, and Reuben. He noticed that Reuben had a revolver thrust behind his belt.

"I ain't as good a shot left-handed as I am with my right," Reuben said when Fargo asked him about the gun. "If I'm careful, though, I can generally come pretty close to what I'm aimin' at. And if any o' them owlhoots come after us again, I'm aimin' to blow their blasted brains out."

Fargo grinned. Reuben's body might be wounded, but not his spirit.

Later, before the wagon train got started again and

before Fargo rode back out to take the lead, Sallie managed to find a moment alone with him. She gave him a rather wistful smile and said quietly, "Skye . . . what I said before about what I'd want to do with you if you came along with us . . . it's not that I've changed my mind, or that I didn't enjoy the time we had together . . ."

"But you've got your hands full right now, what with handling one of the wagons and taking care of Reuben," Fargo finished for her when she hesitated. "Don't worry, Sallie. I understand."

"You do? That's wonderful, Skye. I didn't want to hurt your feelings."

He shook his head. "You haven't."

"Maybe sometime after we get to Topeka . . ."

"Sure," Fargo said, but he didn't really think it was going to happen. He had seen the way Sallie hovered over Reuben, taking care of him and worrying about him, and he had seen as well the way Reuben looked at her.

"Mr. Sanborn is quite a man," Sallie went on after a moment. "Rough around the edges, but a gentleman at heart."

"I reckon that's a pretty good description of him," Fargo agreed.

"He certainly has a lot of amusing stories about the places he's been and the things he's done."

"Like I told you and your pa, Reuben's been to see the elephant. You won't find a better man out here on the frontier."

"Well, I don't know about that. . . ." She came up on her toes and brushed a quick kiss across his lips. "I can think of one who's just as good."

McCabe came along right after that, so they left things as they stood. Fargo was convinced, though, that by the time they reached Topeka, the bond between Sallie and Reuben would have grown strong enough so that she would no longer be thinking about him.

That was just fine with Fargo. He enjoyed his life the way it was, never knowing what—or who—might be waiting for him just over the horizon.

Somewhat to Fargo's surprise, the band of desperadoes that had attacked the wagon train didn't make another try for the precious cargo of supplies. The next four days went by without any trouble, just long, grueling hours of travel across the prairie each day, broken only by a brief stop in the settlement of Lawrence, the halfway point in the journey to Topeka.

While the wagons were stopped, Fargo took Reuben to the office of the town's only doctor to have his wound examined. The doctor examined the injury, and confirmed that Reuben's collarbone was broken. He said that the bullet holes seemed to be healing nicely.

"You've done everything you can for him," the doctor told Fargo. "Just keep that shoulder bound up tightly so that the bone will have a chance to knit properly." To Reuben he said, "You may always have a little pain when you use that arm, my friend, but other than that I think you'll be back to normal in a few months."

"A few months?" Reuben repeated. "I can't be laid up for that long!"

"Why not?" Fargo said. "You didn't plan on heading back to the mountains until next spring anyway, did you?"

"Well, no, but still . . ."

"The rest'll do you good," Fargo told him. "Just take it easy like the doc says."

Reuben grumbled, but he reluctantly agreed to follow the doctor's advice. Fargo figured he would have a little talk with Sallie. She would see to it that Reuben did as he was told.

The wagon train pushed on, and when Fargo came in sight of smoke rising from the chimneys of Topeka late in the afternoon of the sixth day, he felt relief go through him. Now the supplies would get where they were going and help the settlers in Kansas Territory make it through the coming winter.

He galloped back to the lead wagon and said to McCabe, "The town's just a couple of miles ahead. I don't think anybody's going to bother you this close to the settlement, so I'm going to ride on in and let folks know you're coming."

McCabe nodded. "That's a fine idea, Mr. Fargo."

Turning the Ovaro, Fargo rode toward Topeka. Soon he saw the buildings of the town rising from the prairie. Topeka sat on the south bank of the Kansas River, with a main street that ran for several blocks and cross streets lined with houses. Fargo had been there before and thought it was a pleasant little settlement, for the most part. There were a few saloons and whorehouses, of course, the same sort that could be found in any frontier community.

As he rode past a couple of large warehouses on the edge of town he saw that a canvas banner had been stretched across the main street, hung on ropes that ran from the false fronts of two buildings facing each other. The banner was draped with red, white, and blue bunting, and painted on it in large letters were the words WELCOME TO THE FIRST ANNUAL SHAWNEE COUNTY FAIR AND EXTRAVAGANZA.

The town didn't look like any sort of extravaganza was going on. In fact, not many people were moving around on the street.

He saw Professor Spaulding's wagon parked next to the public well at the far end of town. The professor's horses, with their flashy harnesses and plumed head-gear, were nowhere in sight.

As Fargo rode past one of the saloons he heard his name called and looked over to see Spaulding standing in the doorway. The professor stepped out onto the boardwalk and lifted a hand in greeting.

"Glad to see you made it, Professor," Fargo said as he reined in. "Did you have any more trouble along the way?"

"Not a bit," Spaulding replied. He hooked his thumbs in the pockets of his vest.

With a grin, Fargo gestured at the new beaver hat Spaulding wore and commented, "I thought you said there wasn't another hat like that this side of St. Louis."

"What can I say? Dame Fortune smiled on me, my young friend." Spaulding frowned. "I was concerned when you failed to return the next morning after we met on the trail. The chances that some misfortune had befallen you seemed rather high to me."

"Sorry, Professor. I wound up having to lead that wagon train I told you about." Fargo pointed a thumb back down the trail to the east. "It'll be here in a little while, full of provisions and other supplies."

"Excellent! That will help the citizens of this benighted territory endure their hardships until the land once more springs forth in blossoms."

"There won't be any blossoms springing forth without some good rain," Fargo pointed out.

Spaulding made a grandiloquent gesture that ended with him patting himself on the chest. "I will take care of that necessity, my boy," he declared. "In a few days, at the culmination of the Shawnee County Fair, I shall work my cloud wizardry and make the heavens bring forth rain!"

Several passersby had stopped to listen to Spaulding's claims, and now one of the men said, "Just how do you plan on doin' that, mister?"

"I have my own secret processes, developed over years of intensive study," Spaulding replied. He smiled indulgently. "I would explain the scientific intricacies, my good man, but I fear they would be beyond the comprehension of your more rudimentary brain."

"Are you callin' me dumb?" the man responded. He was dressed like a farmer, and a poor one at that, but he had his pride and his eyes flashed angrily.

"Not at all, not at all. I know nothing of your day-to-day work, my friend, just as I expect you know nothing of mine. To each his own, eh?"

That mollified the farmer a little. "Well, if you say so," he replied dubiously. "I still don't see how anybody can *make* it rain, though."

"Keep watching the skies, my friend. Keep watching the skies."

The farmer and his companions, also homesteaders by the looks of them, moved on, muttering and casting suspicious glances at Spaulding. The professor ignored them and flicked an imaginary mote of dust off his lapel.

Fargo hoped for the professor's sake that he didn't turn out to be a charlatan. If folks around here got their hopes up, only to be disappointed when Spaulding failed to make it rain, they might go on a rampage and take out their frustrations on him. He might get his wagon busted up and find himself being tarred and feathered and run out of town on a rail.

Fargo wasn't too sure he would blame the settlers if they did that, either.

Quietly, he asked Spaulding, "Just how *do* you make it rain, Professor?"

"Trade secrets, my boy. Trade secrets. I appreciate

your earlier kindness, of course, but even so, I must be discreet about revealing my methods."

Fargo lifted the Ovaro's reins. "Well, good luck," he said. "I've got to go find a fella named Coleman and talk to him."

"Henry Coleman?" Spaulding asked.

Fargo paused. "That's right. You know him?"

"I met him yesterday when I reached town. He's the owner of this fine establishment behind me, as well as having his fingers in numerous other commercial pies in this fair city."

Fargo lifted his eyes to the sign on the building's false front. THE GRAND KANSAS SALOON, it read. H. COLEMAN, PROP.

"Looks like I'll have to have a drink," he said as he swung down from the saddle.

"And I'll join you, of course. Thank you for your kind invitation, Mr. Fargo."

Fargo didn't recall issuing any invitation, but he didn't argue. Since Spaulding already knew Coleman, having the professor along might come in handy. He tied the Ovaro to the hitch rail and stepped into the saloon.

5

The Grand Kansas Saloon was a large building with a long hardwood bar on the left side of the room, tables scattered across the floor, and a piano on the right-hand wall between two large windows. These windows made the place brighter and sunnier than most saloons Fargo had been in.

A poker game was going on at one of the tables. A few men were clustered around a faro layout at the back of the room. Half a dozen men stood at the bar drinking.

Spaulding led Fargo past the bar toward a table where a man in a brown tweed suit sat dealing a hand of solitaire. "Mr. Coleman," Spaulding said, "I have someone here who wants to meet you."

Coleman looked up from his cards. He was a dapper, thin-faced man with a shock of graying sandy hair and a mustache. His deep-set eyes lit up with interest as he saw the big, buckskin-clad man with Spaulding.

The professor went on, "Mr. Fargo, meet Mr. Henry Coleman. Mr. Coleman, Mr. Skye Fargo."

"Mr. Fargo!" Coleman said as he came to his feet and extended his hand. He was as tall as Fargo. "I had about given up hope of meeting you. I was afraid something must have happened to you on your way here."

"I got delayed a couple of times," Fargo replied as

he shook hands with the saloonkeeper. "What can I do for you?"

"Right down to business, eh?" Coleman said with a grin. "I like that. Sit down, sit down. We'll have a drink as we talk." He signaled to an aproned man working behind the bar.

That sounded all right to Fargo. It had been a week since Fargo had had a drink of anything stronger than water, and he realized now that he was thirsty.

The three men sat down, Spaulding continuing to invite himself to be a part of this discussion. If Coleman didn't mind, neither did Fargo. He had no secrets. He was just here to listen to whatever Coleman had to say.

The bartender brought over a bottle and three glasses and poured the drinks. Coleman lifted his glass and said, "To profitable business ventures, gentlemen."

"I'd rather drink to the end of the awful drought afflicting this unfortunate territory," Spaulding said.

Coleman smiled. "Well, I can't argue with that. To the end of the drought."

Fargo drank with the others, enjoying the warmth that the whiskey brought to his belly. As he set the empty glass on the table, he said again, "What can I do for you, Mr. Coleman?" He shook his head when Coleman offered to refill his drink. The professor accepted.

"Well, as you now know, Mr. Fargo, I'm the owner of the Grand Kansas Saloon." Coleman waved a slender hand at the room around them. "This is not my only business investment in Topeka, however. I also own the best hotel, the largest livery stable, and the town's leading mercantile emporium."

Fargo didn't say anything, but his mind was working. The situation Coleman described wasn't that uncommon. A man could come into a new settlement—especially a man with money—and quickly establish himself as the leading businessman. Sometimes that worked out well, but often it didn't, as that much power and money often made a man greedier for both of those things. He reserved judgment on Henry Coleman, though, because certainly not every businessman was that way.

"Did you notice a pair of large warehouses on your way into town?" Coleman went on.

Fargo nodded. "I did."

"Those are mine as well. I use them to store the goods and supplies that I sell in the emporium."

A frown creased Fargo's forehead. "I thought there was a shortage of supplies in the territory right now."

"What gave you that idea? My warehouses are almost full, and I'm expecting more supplies in another week or two."

"I came most of the way from Missouri with a wagon train carrying supplies that were donated by churches back east," Fargo explained. "The people with the wagons are bringing the supplies out here to help people get through these hard times."

Coleman shook his head. "There's no need for that. At least in this area I'm having no trouble supplying the needs of the settlers."

"Free of charge?" Fargo asked.

"Well, of course not. Every businessman is entitled to an honest profit, after all."

Fargo was beginning to get a bad feeling about this. He said, "Why exactly did you ask me to come out here, Mr. Coleman?"

The saloonkeeper leaned forward. "I've heard of you, Mr. Fargo," he said. "I'm told you're a tough man and a good hand with a gun. Also that you're the best guide and scout on the frontier. Some people call you the Trailsman, I believe."

"Go on," Fargo said tightly.

"Very well. I won't lie to you, Mr. Fargo, some people seem to resent my success. They look on my business enterprises, especially my warehouses, with envy. I've had to post guards in them around the clock, just to prevent wholesale thievery."

"You don't need me to stand guard for you in a warehouse," Fargo said.

"Indeed not. There are plenty of men who can handle that chore. I told you that I have more supplies coming in. I'd like for you to ride back to Missouri, meet my wagon train, and guide it here, making sure that it arrives safely."

"That's what I just did with that other supply train," Fargo pointed out.

A smile curved Coleman's thin lips. "Yes, but I'll pay you well for your services, instead of expecting you to risk your life out of the goodness of your heart." Coleman poured himself another drink. "And once this job is done, there'll be others like it. I have good contacts back east, and I expect to bring in a steady stream of supplies."

"To sell for a profit," Fargo said.

"Naturally."

"How much of a profit?"

"I beg your pardon?" Coleman said.

"I asked how much of a profit you intend to make on those supplies."

For the first time, Coleman's polite, friendly pose slipped a little. "I don't see how that's any of your concern," he said.

"These settlers have had a hard time of it. I don't want to see anybody taking advantage of them on the prices of the things they need to get by."

"Oh, in that case," and Coleman waved a hand negligently, "don't worry about it, Mr. Fargo. I'm always happy to extend credit to anyone who needs it."

Fargo's mouth tightened. That was the last nail in the coffin, as far as he was concerned. He saw what was going on here, and he was sorry that he had ever taken Coleman's one hundred dollars.

That could be remedied. He still had the money. He could return it and walk out of here with a clear conscience, even though that would leave him almost broke. Better that than to have money from a man like Coleman in his poke.

"Well, Mr. Fargo," Coleman said with a smile, "what do you say?"

Before Fargo could reply, the door of the saloon opened and a man stepped inside, moving fast. He spotted Coleman sitting with Fargo and Spaulding in the rear of the room, and he strode angrily toward the table.

"Coleman!" he said sharply. "I've got a bone to pick with you."

Coleman looked up and sighed as he recognized the newcomer. "Ainsley," he said as if the name tasted bad in his mouth. "You always have a bone to pick. What is it this time?"

"Jed Carrothers," the man called Ainsley snapped. He was in his thirties, brown-haired and handsome in a rough-hewn way. He wore black trousers, a white shirt, and a black vest, with a ribbon tie cinched around his neck.

Fargo took note of the dark stains on Ainsley's fingers and knew right away what profession the man practiced. Sometimes he thought that newspapermen were said to have printer's ink in their blood because they got so much on their hands some of it had to soak in.

"What about Carrothers?" Coleman asked.

"You know what I'm talking about. He's packing up and leaving his place. He came by to tell me."

66

Coleman shrugged. "Why is that any business of mine? These homesteaders abandon their farms all the time."

"And you're right there to take them over, aren't you?" Ainsley accused.

Coleman began gathering up the cards he had spread out earlier. "It's true that Carrothers owed me quite a bill at my store. He came to me and offered to settle up, his farm for what he owed me. Yes, I took it, but it was a bad deal on my part. What good is a dried-up homestead to me?"

"It won't be dried up forever, and you know it! And it's not the first farm you've taken over like that, not by a long shot. When the drought breaks—"

"*If* the drought breaks," Coleman put in.

"When the drought breaks," Ainsley went on stubbornly, "you'll own every bit of decent farmland in the whole county! It's not enough you own half the town. You have to get your filthy paws on everything else that's worth anything!"

Ainsley's voice had risen as he spoke, until he was shouting. All conversation in the saloon had stopped. Everyone stared at the confrontation going on at the rear table.

Coleman didn't seem upset, despite the newspaperman's accusations. "You're making a scene, Ainsley," he said with a note of mocking humor in his drawl. "Aren't you embarrassed for yourself?"

"No, what I am is good and mad. I've stood by and watched you and your bullyboys run roughshod over this town, and I don't intend to stand by and watch you take over the entire county."

Coleman looked across the table at Fargo and smiled. He still had no idea that Fargo's opinion of him was every bit as low as Ainsley's, if not lower.

"I'm sorry about this interruption, Mr. Fargo," he

said. "Our young firebrand of an editor here tends to get carried away. Let me deal with him, and then you and I will get back to our business."

Fargo was about to tell Coleman that they didn't have any business to discuss, but before he could say anything the saloonkeeper made a curt gesture and two men stood up from a nearby table. Fargo had noticed them when he came in with Spaulding, but he hadn't paid any attention to them since. Both men were burly and wore range clothes. Their faces were cold and hard as they approached the table.

Hardcases, Fargo thought. Hired guns. The bullyboys that Ainsley had spoken of. Without a doubt they were about to grab the newspaperman and throw him out of the Grand Kansas Saloon.

At least, that was the plan.

Fargo came to his feet, taking Coleman by surprise. He reached under his shirt and took out the small leather poke that hung by a strip of rawhide around his neck. Coleman motioned for his men to wait while he looked curiously at Fargo.

The Trailsman opened the poke and took out the small roll of greenbacks. He dropped them on the table in front of Coleman and said, "There's your money back. I don't have any interest in working for you, Coleman."

The dapper saloonkeeper frowned. "Are you sure, Mr. Fargo? I must say, I'm disappointed that you're not even giving me a chance to persuade you otherwise."

"I've heard enough," Fargo said. "More than enough."

He saw the icy glitter in Coleman's eyes and knew that he had made an enemy. Fargo didn't care. He didn't like Coleman, didn't have any use for what the man was doing here in Topeka.

"You're sure?" Coleman asked softly.

"Positive."

Ainsley didn't like being ignored. He said, "I'm not done with you, Coleman."

"Oh, yes, you are." Coleman flipped his hand toward Ainsley, signaling his men to move in.

Fargo moved smoothly around the table, taking up a position beside Ainsley.

"Oh, my," Professor Spaulding said. "Oh, my."

The newspaperman glanced at him, curious but grateful for the help. Fargo gave him a nod.

The odds were even now, which made Coleman's men hesitate for a second. But they couldn't back down in front of their boss, so with snarls of anger they charged Fargo and Ainsley.

Fargo took a quick step to the side so that the men couldn't bull-rush over both of them. The man coming at him threw a punch. Fargo blocked it easily and sent a right cross into the man's jaw like a blue whistler. The blow landed solidly and made the man's knees unhinge. He went down, and wrapped his arms around Fargo's knees. Fargo felt his legs jerked out from under him. He fell, knocking aside an empty chair as he did so.

"Be careful!" Coleman called over the clamor of the fight. "Not too much damage!"

Fargo didn't know how the newspaperman was doing, but he heard grunts of effort and the meaty thud of fists striking flesh and bone. Fargo's own hands were full at the moment. The man who had tackled him scrambled up and lunged toward him, aiming his knee at Fargo's groin. Fargo twisted aside and the man's knee struck his hip. The impact was painful, but he stood his ground.

The man's hands clawed at Fargo's throat, trying to get a grip so that he could choke the life out of the

Trailsman. Fargo cupped his hands and clapped them over the man's ears. The concussive force of the air popped the man's eardrums and made him howl in pain. Fargo grabbed his shirt and threw him to the side.

Unfortunately, he heaved the man right into the legs of Ainsley, who was still trading punches with his opponent. Struck from behind, Ainsley fell over backward and landed in a tangled heap with the man Fargo had been fighting.

Fargo wasn't particular about his opponent. He rolled over, got a hand on the floor, and surged up to confront the man Ainsley had been battling. He ducked a punch, blocked another, and then hooked a left to the body and a right jab to the face. The man stumbled back a couple of steps.

Pressing his advantage, Fargo bored in, throwing rights and lefts until a roundhouse right connected and knocked the man back onto a table. The legs of the table snapped under the weight, collapsing the whole thing. The man lay there in the wreckage, stunned and moaning, no longer a threat.

Fargo swung around to see that Ainsley was sitting on top of the other man, holding him by the throat and bouncing his head up and down on the floor. The man was out cold by now, but Ainsley wasn't letting up.

Quickly, Fargo stepped over and gripped the newspaperman's shoulder. "Take it easy!" he said sharply. "You're going to kill him if you're not careful."

Ainsley stopped slamming the man's head against the floor. He stared down at his opponent, blinking rapidly and looking confused, almost as if he didn't know what was going on. Fargo realized the newspaperman had been caught up in the grip of a frenzied, killing rage.

He let go of the man's neck and jerked his hands back as if he had been holding a snake. He stood up, clearly shaken, and passed a hand over his eyes.

"I'll have both of you arrested," Henry Coleman's voice lashed at Fargo and Ainsley. "Look at the damage you've caused in my saloon!"

"We just defended ourselves," Fargo said coldly.

"No," Ainsley choked out. "No, he's right, damn him. This is Coleman's place, and he has a right to have anybody thrown out if he wants to. You don't have to summon the sheriff, Coleman. We'll turn ourselves in."

Fargo frowned. He wasn't in the habit of apologizing for his actions when somebody else threw the first punch, and he sure as hell didn't intend to go to jail for it. Ainsley could be that stiff-necked and self-righteous if he wanted to, but it wasn't Fargo's way.

Coleman sneered at Ainsley's offer. "You don't think I'll take your word for that, do you? I've already sent for the sheriff."

Sure enough, at that moment the door of the saloon opened and a big man hurried in, a star pinned to his wool shirt under a sheepskin jacket. He had a rawboned face under a battered old hat, and he demanded in a high-pitched twang, "Just what in blue blazes is goin' on here?"

Fargo turned to look at the lawman, but his attention was caught by the woman who hurried into the saloon right behind the sheriff. She wore a dark blue dress that failed to conceal the abundant curves of her body. Her eyes were dark blue, too, almost matching her dress, and her hair was black as a raven's wing. She stepped around the sheriff and practically ran toward Fargo and Ainsley.

"Thomas!" she exclaimed anxiously. "Thomas, are you all right?"

So it wasn't him she was worried about but rather Ainsley, Fargo thought wryly. Well, that came as no surprise, considering that he had never seen her before. She was pretty enough that he knew he would have remembered her.

Ainsley caught hold of her arms. "I'm fine, Diane," he told her. "A little disheveled, that's all."

She touched a small cut above his eye, a souvenir of one of the punches that had landed on him. "You're bleeding," she said.

"It's nothing," Ainsley insisted.

Coleman was on his feet now. He stalked toward the sheriff and pointed at Fargo and Ainsley.

"Sheriff, I want you to arrest those two for brawling, disturbing the peace, and destruction of private property!"

The lawman thumbed back his hat. "Well, now, I don't know that I can do that," he said. "Miss Diane fetched me first. She said Tom and some other fella were about to be assaulted in here for no good reason."

"My men had every reason to try to throw them out. They were making a disturbance."

"Seems to me we were just talking," Fargo said.

The sheriff held up a hand. "I'll get to you in a minute, mister. Right now I'm listenin' to Mr. Coleman."

Fargo wondered if the lawman was actually in Coleman's pocket. It wouldn't be unusual for the local law to be under the control of the town's wealthiest, most powerful businessman. The whole situation in Topeka stunk to high heaven.

"I reckon you got a right to put folks out of your place," the sheriff went on to Coleman, "but you can't have your boys beat on 'em for no good reason. Now, if Tom and this stranger were puttin' up a fuss . . ."

"That's exactly what happened," Coleman snapped. "I asked them to leave, and they started fighting with my men."

He looked around the room, as if daring anyone to disagree with him.

"Actually . . ." The voice spoke up tentatively. Fargo glanced around and saw that Professor Spaulding had finally gotten to his feet. Spaulding cleared his throat and went on. "Actually, while it's true that this ink-stained representative of the fourth estate waxed eloquently with some rather heated verbiage, the first individuals to employ physical violence were the two myrmidons of Mr. Coleman there. The, ah, unconscious ones."

The sheriff frowned. "I reckon that was English, but I'm damned if I know what you just said, Professor."

"Coleman's men threw the first punches," Fargo translated. "Ainsley and I were just defending ourselves."

"Is that right?"

"Everyone here saw it, Sheriff," Ainsley said. "Ask them somewhere Coleman can't intimidate them. You'll get the truth then."

"Well, I don't know that I've got the time for some big fancy investigation. . . ." The sheriff looked around the room. The only real damage was the broken table. "I reckon twenty dollars will cover the tab for what got busted up. There won't be no charges. No need to bother the judge with a little fracas like this."

"But, Sheriff—" Coleman began.

"Twenty dollars will cover it," the sheriff said again, his affable tone hardening a little now.

Coleman didn't like it, but he wasn't willing to press the issue. He jerked his head in a nod and said, "Very well. Twenty dollars for the damages."

Fargo reached for his poke. Paying his share of the

money would clean him out good and proper, but there was nothing else he could do.

Ainsley stopped him with an upheld hand. "Forget it, friend," he said. "I'll take care of this."

"I pay my own way," Fargo said.

"So do I. And this wasn't your fight."

Maybe it hadn't started out that way, Fargo thought, but as he looked at the hatred glittering icily in Coleman's eyes, he knew that he was sure as hell part of it now.

Ainsley took out a twenty-dollar gold piece and tossed it on the floor at Coleman's feet. "There's your money," he said. "That's all you'll ever get from me, Coleman."

"You may sing a different tune when you're hungry enough," Coleman said.

"I'll starve to death before I spend a penny in your store." Ainsley took the woman's arm. "Come on, Diane. Let's get out of here."

Spaulding came hurriedly around the table. "I believe that I, ah, will accompany you." He cast a worried glance at Coleman, who was staring coldly at him. Going against the saloonkeeper couldn't have been easy for the professor, Fargo thought. He wondered why Spaulding had done it.

Fargo started toward the door. Coleman surprised him by saying, "I'm sorry we couldn't do business together, Mr. Fargo. I think we would have made quite a formidable team."

"Not in this life," Fargo said with a shake of his head.

He stepped out onto the boardwalk behind the others. Before he could go anywhere, though, the sheriff followed him out of the saloon. "Hold on there a minute, mister. I want to talk to you."

Fargo faced the lawman squarely and asked, "What can I do for you, Sheriff?"

"First off, tell me who you are. I don't recollect seein' you around Topeka before."

"That's because I just rode in. My name's Fargo."

"He's Skye Fargo," Spaulding spoke up.

"The Trailsman?" Ainsley said, sounding surprised. "I've seen stories about you in newspapers and in *Harper's Weekly*."

"Yeah, I reckon I've heard of you, too," the sheriff said as he rubbed his jaw. "What brings you to Topeka?"

"I'm with a wagon train full of supplies that ought to be rolling into town any time now," Fargo explained.

"Not one of Coleman's wagon trains?" Ainsley asked.

Fargo shook his head. "No, this one is led by a preacher named Joshua McCabe. It was put together by church folks who wanted to donate supplies and help out the settlers here in Kansas Territory. People back east have heard about how bad the drought has been."

"Well, what do you know about that!" the sheriff said. "That's mighty nice of 'em. But what was that Mr. Coleman said about you and him doin' business together?"

"Coleman wanted me to take over the job of bringing in supplies for him to sell in his store. He wrote to me and asked me to come see him, even paid me for my time and trouble in getting here."

"That was the money you returned to him," Spaulding guessed.

Fargo nodded. "I don't want to work for him, and I didn't want to keep his money."

"So that's why you helped me?" Ainsley asked. "You don't like Coleman?"

"That's part of it," Fargo agreed. "But mainly I just don't like to see a fight where the odds aren't even."

"Things are never even around here," Ainsley said bitterly. "The odds are always stacked in Coleman's favor. No one wants to stand up to the gunmen who work for him."

The sheriff said, "Dang it, it ain't all that bad, Tom. I enforce the law the best I can and try to treat everybody fair and square."

"I know you do, Sheriff, but you're only one man. No one expects you to be able to fight an army, and that's just about what Coleman has in Brinker and his bunch."

Fargo stiffened. "Brinker, did you say?"

Ainsley looked at him and nodded. "That's right, Jed Brinker. He heads up the gun crew that works for Coleman. Do you know him?"

"I know him," Fargo said slowly.

And remembering what had happened between him and Brinker the first time they met, Fargo knew for sure now that he was in this fight. He was in it right up to his neck.

6

Before the group standing on the boardwalk outside the Grand Kansas Saloon could discuss the situation in Topeka any further, a commotion rose on the eastern outskirts of town. Fargo looked down the street in that direction.

"Here come those wagons I was telling you about," he said.

He was glad to see that the supply train had covered the remaining distance into town without any more trouble. He hadn't expected any problems and would have been surprised if anyone had tried to stop the group while it was so close to Topeka.

The conversation with Henry Coleman had given Fargo quite a bit to think about, including the possible identities of the men who had attacked the wagons. He put that speculation aside for the moment, and led the little group with him down the street to meet the wagons.

A crowd was gathering already. On the driver's box in the lead, Joshua McCabe called answers to the shouted questions, explaining that he and his companions had brought supplies. That news brought whoops of excitement from some of the onlookers.

McCabe saw Fargo coming toward him and grinned. "Praise the Lord!" he called. "We made it, Mr. Fargo! We made it!"

Fargo nodded and said, "I knew you would."

"Dadgum it," the sheriff put in. "I'm gonna have a riot on my hands here in a minute if these folks don't settle down." To McCabe, he said, "You best get these wagons parked somewhere."

"We'll set up at one of the local churches," McCabe said.

The sheriff pointed. "The Baptist church is the closest, right down the street. Head for there!"

Fargo saw that the sheriff was right: trouble might be brewing. Supplies had been scarce for months. Some of the townspeople were hungry, and the homesteaders who happened to be in Topeka today were probably in even worse shape. Men ran up to the wagons and started pulling at the canvas covers over the beds. If they pulled those covers off, revealing the contents of the wagons, the temptation might be too much to resist. They might start looting.

The second wagon, the one driven by Sallie McCabe, came abreast of Fargo. He caught hold and pulled himself up to stand on the box beside her. Reuben was propped up in the back, sitting in a little nest made for him in the center of the supplies. He had a pistol in his left hand and looked worried that the situation was going to get out of hand.

Fargo felt sorry for the people of Topeka. The drought had been no fault of theirs, and they had suffered for months. Still, he wasn't going to allow them to loot the wagons just because he was sympathetic to their plight. He slipped the Colt from its holster, and squeezed off two rounds into the air.

The roar of the shots made people freeze. All eyes turned to Fargo as the wagons drew to a lurching halt.

"Everybody settle down!" Fargo shouted. "There's enough to go around and to help everyone, but not if you get carried away and start grabbing everything you see! The wagons will be parked down at the Baptist church. You can come there later, and the supplies will be distributed fairly and evenly."

There were rumbles of resentment and discontent, but the sight of Fargo standing there on the wagon, gun in hand, was enough to make people think twice about defying him.

The sheriff clambered up on McCabe's wagon and added his voice. "Everybody clear out!" he bellowed. "Come to the church later, like that fella said, and you'll get what you need! Now back off and let these wagons through!"

Grudgingly the crowd parted, and people stopped pawing at the canvas covers and the supplies underneath them. Fargo stayed where he was, gun drawn, as the wagons began to roll again.

"I thought for a minute that was gonna turn ugly, Skye," Reuben said.

"So did I."

"I'm mighty glad you came along when you did."

"I am, too, Skye," Sallie said. "You can't blame people for being desperate when they find themselves in desperate circumstances, but they have to be patient."

It was hard to be patient when your belly was in a knot because it was empty, Fargo thought, but he knew Sallie was right. It would take time to distribute the supplies fairly.

Fargo had lost track of Ainsley and Diane, but a moment later the wagons passed a building with a sign that read TOPEKA CLARION. He saw Ainsley hurrying inside. Diane paused on the boardwalk and looked up at Fargo with speculation and interest in her dark blue eyes.

That made his jaw tighten with concern. Not that he didn't appreciate it when any attractive woman looked at him like that, but he guessed Diane was Thomas Ainsley's wife, and Fargo wasn't the sort to jump another man's claim. He had gotten involved with married women in the past, but only under very special circumstances.

The wagons moved on down the street to the church and parked in a vacant lot beside it. The local minister came out of the parsonage behind the church and hurried up to talk to McCabe and the sheriff.

Fargo hopped down from the box and turned to help Sallie climb to the ground. She stretched, glad for the chance to ease muscles made sore by long days of driving.

"Give me a hand here, Skye," Reuben said. "I'm getting around a little better now, but I still need some help gettin' in and out of this wagon."

Fargo took hold of Reuben's arm to steady the big mountain man as he clambered out of the wagon. Joshua McCabe came up to them and said, "Thank you, Mr. Fargo. Things were about to get out of hand when you stepped in."

"They'll be all right now," Fargo said. "Folks were just getting carried away and not stopping to think."

The sheriff walked up and introduced himself to McCabe. "Avery Tucker," he said as he shook hands with the burly preacher. "Welcome to Topeka."

"I'm Joshua McCabe, this is my daughter Sallie, and our friend Reuben Sanborn. I suppose you already know Mr. Fargo here."

Tucker nodded and gave Fargo a narrow-eyed glance. "Uh-huh. I wouldn't mind havin' a mite more palaver with you, either, Fargo."

"Sure, Sheriff," Fargo agreed. "I'm a little busy right now, though, what with getting everything squared away here."

McCabe said, "Oh, don't worry about that. Your

task was to get us here safely, Mr. Fargo. You've accomplished that, so let us worry about the rest of it."

"Yeah, I'll keep an eye on things, Skye," Reuben added.

Fargo nodded. "In that case, Sheriff, I'll go with you right now. There are a few things I want to talk to you about, too."

They left the bustle of activity around the church and walked back down the street. The crowd had dispersed somewhat, but there were still a few sullen people milling around.

"That fella McCabe better post himself some guards tonight," Tucker muttered under his breath to Fargo as they moved on.

"He's used to protecting his cargo," Fargo said. "That cost him some men the first night on the trail, though."

Tucker glanced sharply at him. "What's that?"

"The wagons were attacked by night riders. They were trying to steal the supplies, but when those good folks started shooting back, they tried to set fire to them instead."

Tucker frowned and said, "I reckon I can see why somebody might want to steal supplies. The way things are in the territory, a sack o' flour is might' near as good as gold. But why in blazes would anybody try to destroy something that folks need so bad?"

"I've got an idea about that," Fargo said. "I'd rather get off the street before I go into it, though."

Not only that, but he also wasn't sure just how much he could trust Sheriff Avery Tucker. The lawman seemed honest and aboveboard, but that could be a pose.

Thomas Ainsley had been watching them through the window in the front of the newspaper office. As they passed the *Clarion* Ainsley stepped out and said,

"Sheriff, why don't you and Mr. Fargo step inside? I'd like to thank Mr. Fargo for his help, and Diane is about to put supper on the table."

Tucker's rather homely face lit up with a smile. "Now, you know an old bachelor like me don't never turn down a home-cooked meal, Tom. If it's all right with Fargo here . . ."

Fargo nodded. He had a feeling that between Ainsley and the sheriff, he could find out everything he needed to know about what was going on in Topeka these days. If Ainsley trusted Tucker, that was probably a good indication that Fargo could, too.

"That would be fine," he said. "I've been on the trail for a week, so a meal with a roof over my head would be mighty enjoyable."

When the three men stepped inside, Fargo saw that Professor Spaulding was already there, looking over the sheets of newsprint that were pinned on one wall. They were the front pages of numerous issues of the Topeka *Clarion*. A couple of desks sat in the front of the room, and beyond them, behind a railing, was the press area, with the big mechanical contraption taking up most of the space. A door in a corner led into what was evidently living quarters.

The smell of food mingled with the sharp tang of printer's ink.

Diane appeared in the doorway and smiled at the men. "Dinner is ready," she announced.

They followed her down a hallway to a roomy kitchen with a large table in the middle of it. On the table was a pot of stew and a plate with a few biscuits on it. Fargo frowned as he realized that these folks didn't have an abundance of food. They were willing to share what they had, though.

"No offense, ma'am," he said to Diane, "but I'm

not all that hungry. I'll just have a small bowl of stew, if that's all right with you."

"Same here," Sheriff Tucker said, picking up on what Fargo meant.

Professor Spaulding patted his well-fed paunch. "And as you can observe, it would be best for me to partake only lightly as well, though the aroma is so delicious I am mightily tempted."

Diane flushed faintly as she nodded. "Of course, gentlemen. Just eat what you want."

She ladled out bowls of stew and passed them around the table as the men sat down, taking her own bowl last. Ainsley sat at the head of the table, with Diane and Fargo to his right, Spaulding and the sheriff to his left. They dug in, and Fargo had to admit that although there wasn't much food, what there was of it was mighty good. Clearly, in these times of scarcity Diane had learned to make do.

There wasn't much conversation while they were eating. It wasn't until the last bit of stew had been sopped up with biscuits that Sheriff Tucker broached the subject that was on his mind.

"Just what's the connection between you and Jed Brinker, Fargo?" he asked. "I could see you wasn't too happy when his name came up earlier."

"Brinker and I had a run-in over in Missouri," Fargo explained. "He didn't take it kindly, and I think he and a friend of his tried to bushwhack me later."

"You mean they attempted to kill you?" Ainsley said.

"That's right. A couple of men took some shots at me, and I suspect one of them was Brinker."

"Thank God they didn't hurt you," Diane said.

Fargo nodded. "I was lucky, all right. But that's not all. Remember, Sheriff, what I told you about night riders attacking that wagon train?"

Tucker said, "Sure. It still don't make a lot of sense to me, though."

"I'm getting to that," Fargo said. "But the first thing is that I heard the boss of those outlaws shouting commands at them. His voice sounded a little familiar at the time, but I couldn't place it. Now that I've thought about it, I'm pretty sure the man was Jed Brinker. It took me a while to come up with that, because I hadn't heard Brinker talk all that much, and besides his voice was muffled by a mask during the attack on the wagons."

Tucker slapped a hand down on the table. "Brinker!" he exclaimed. "Damned if I don't believe it!" He glanced at Diane. "Pardon my language, ma'am."

"Don't worry about that, Sheriff," she told him with a smile. "I'm no shrinking violet. My brother and I have been in the newspaper business too long for that."

Fargo looked at her. Thomas Ainsley was her *brother*? Fargo had taken them for husband and wife, but now as he thought back on it, there hadn't been any real indication of that. Diane had been worried about Ainsley when she came into the saloon after the brawl, but it was just as natural for a sister to be worried about her brother as it was for a wife to be concerned about her husband.

That put a different face on things, but Fargo couldn't really spend a lot of time pondering the possibilities now. He wanted to get the rest of his thoughts in order.

"Brinker works for Henry Coleman," Ainsley said. "Why would Coleman order Brinker and his gunmen to attack that wagon train, unless . . ."

"Unless Coleman wanted those supplies for himself," Fargo finished. "Coleman said he has a wagon train of his own coming in soon. If Brinker and his gunnies had wiped out Reverend McCabe and his men, they could have taken over the wagons, joined up with Coleman's train, and come on into Topeka without anybody knowing the difference."

Tucker rubbed his bristly jaw in thought. "I reckon that makes sense, Fargo. But why have Brinker try to burn up the supplies if he couldn't steal 'em?"

"I can answer that," Ainsley said. "Because Coleman doesn't want any competition. Remember what happened to Walt Tyson, Sheriff?"

Tucker nodded grimly. "I sure do."

"Who's Tyson?" Fargo asked.

"Fella who owned a freight company," the lawman explained. "He was bringin' in supplies from Missouri, until one night his barn burned down—with him in it."

"Everyone thought it was an accident," Diane said.

"Not everyone," Ainsley said. "Some of us believed that Coleman had something to do with the fire. Right after it happened he raised prices again in his store."

Fargo said, "Aren't there any other stores in Topeka?"

"A few," Ainsley replied with a shrug. "But they have mostly empty shelves now. They haven't been able to replenish their supplies. Even when the merchants can scrape up enough money to order more goods, most of the shipments never get here for one reason or the other. Some of them simply disappear."

"They disappear," Fargo said, "and then wind up in those warehouses Coleman owns."

The sheriff looked back and forth between Fargo and Ainsley. "You're sayin' that Henry Coleman is nothin' but a thief and a murderer, that he's takin' advantage of the drought to make himself a rich man."

"That's what I've been saying for a long time," Ainsley replied.

Tucker looked at Fargo and said, "You just rode into town a couple of hours ago. How'd you size up Coleman so fast?"

"I've seen setups like this before. Coleman is rich and powerful to start with, but he thinks that if he corners the market on food and other supplies, he'll become even richer. To do that he's got to make sure no one cuts into his operation."

Tucker shook his head slowly. "A fella would have to be a powerful mean polecat to do a thing like that."

Spaulding spoke up, saying, "From what I have observed of Mr. Henry Coleman, Sheriff, that description is a perfect fit for him."

Fargo looked across the table at the professor. "You made an enemy of him, too, when you spoke up for Tom and me. Why did you do that, Professor?"

Spaulding frowned and toyed with his spoon. After a moment he said, "I'm not a man who possesses an abundance of physical courage, Mr. Fargo. I know this about myself and have always been prepared to live with the consequences of it. However, you saved me from those ruffians who were trying to kill me, and therefore I owed you a debt. I am a man who settles his debts fairly and promptly." After a second, Spaulding went on. "Besides, knowing what I know now about Coleman, I believe he may have had some involvement with the attempt on my life."

"Hold on a blasted minute," Sheriff Tucker said. "Why would Coleman try to stop a rainmaker from comin' to town?"

Spaulding spread his pudgy fingers. "Why, it's quite simple, Sheriff. Coleman's scheme to sell supplies to the citizens at obscenely exorbitant prices depends entirely upon the continuation of the unfortunate weather conditions that have settled up Kansas Territory."

"You mean Coleman won't get as rich if the drought breaks?"

"Precisely. And the drought *will* break if I am allowed to perform my cloud wizardry."

"Well, son of a gun," Tucker said. "I reckon you might be on to somethin' there."

Ainsley said, "The question now is what are we going to do about it?"

"We don't have any proof of Coleman's involvement with any of the trouble," Fargo said. "If we did, the sheriff here could contact the nearest U.S. marshal's office and ask for help."

Tucker snorted. "You get me the proof, and I'll arrest Coleman my own self. He's been lordin' it over ever'body in town since he got here, and there ain't nothin' I'd like better than throwin' him behind bars."

"You wouldn't be any match for Brinker and all of his gunmen, Sheriff," Ainsley pointed out.

"I got a couple o' deputies—"

"Both of whom are homesteaders whose farms failed," Ainsley said. "They're good men, Sheriff, but they're not gunslingers."

Fargo asked, "What about the townspeople? Coleman is bound to have some enemies among them."

"I reckon the town's about split," Tucker said. "There's plenty of folks who don't like Coleman, but there's some that do. He's been good for business in Topeka. And there's a heap of folks who'd be flat-out scared to cross him, and I don't reckon you can blame 'em for that."

"But you could find more men you could deputize if you needed them."

"Some," Tucker said with a shrug.

"And McCabe and his men will be in town for a few days," Fargo went on. "McCabe's tough, and so is my friend Reuben, even though he's still laid up from a wound he received when those men raided the wagon train. I think we could put together a force big enough to stand up to Coleman and Brinker."

"I can't do a thing without proof, though," Tucker said. "I may look like a pretty disreputable ol' fella, but when I pinned on this badge I swore to do things legal-like."

Fargo nodded. "I understand that, Sheriff. I'll just have to see what I can do about getting you the proof you need."

"This isn't your fight, Mr. Fargo," Ainsley said. "Why are you so eager to be part of it?"

Fargo smiled thinly and nodded toward Spaulding. "Like the professor, I'm a man who settles his debts. I haven't forgotten being bushwhacked. Not only that, but Reuben was wounded and three men were killed in the attack on those wagons. Somebody's got to pay for that."

"Well, I must say I'm glad you're on our side."

"So am I," Diane added.

Fargo saw that spark of interest in her eyes again. That was one more reason to deal with the threat of Henry Coleman and Jed Brinker as soon as possible. He wanted to get to know Diane Ainsley better.

"You realize, of course," Spaulding said, "that in a few days most of this will be moot?"

"What do you mean, Professor?" Ainsley asked.

"Once it begins to rain, the prairie will bloom and soon Kansas Territory will once again become a land of milk and honey."

Tucker said, "You're mighty dadgummed certain you can make it rain, Professor."

"Of course I can." Spaulding smiled. "I am the Cloud Wizard, am I not?"

*　　*　　*

A little later that evening, after leaving the *Clarion* office, Fargo walked along the street with Sheriff Tucker and Professor Spaulding. The sheriff asked, "You got a place to stay, Fargo?"

"I'd planned on getting a hotel room," Fargo replied with a chuckle. "But giving Coleman back his money left me a little short."

"You're more than welcome to spread your bedroll under my wagon, Mr. Fargo," Spaulding offered. "That's what I do."

"All right, thanks," Fargo said. "I'm obliged for the hospitality, Professor."

Tucker stopped at the squarish stone building that housed his office and the jail. "I meant what I said about arrestin' Coleman," he said to Fargo. "I just got to have the proof first."

The Trailsman nodded. "I'll see what I can do about that."

He and Spaulding strolled on down the street. The professor removed a cigar from his breast pocket and lit up. Fargo shook his head when Spaulding offered him one.

The Ovaro was still tied at the hitching rail in front of Coleman's saloon. Fargo would have worried about leaving the stallion there now that he had made an enemy of Coleman, if he hadn't known that the Ovaro wouldn't allow anyone to mount him. Anybody trying to steal the stallion or even pilfer through Fargo's gear would find himself dodging iron-shod hooves and sharp teeth.

The Ovaro needed to be bedded down for the night, though, so Fargo paused in front of the Grand Kansas Saloon long enough to untie the reins. Several men came out the front door of the building, talking and laughing among themselves. They stopped short when they saw Fargo and Spaulding standing there. The light from the saloon spilled through the front windows and provided plenty of illumination.

The man in the lead of the little group was Jed Brinker. With him were three of the hardcases who had backed him up in Missouri. Glaring, Brinker said, "I heard you were in town, Fargo. If you know what's good for you, you'll light a shuck outta here without wasting any time."

"Well, that's just it," Fargo said, his voice deceptively mild. "I never have known what was good for me. I know what's *not* good for me, though, and that's a couple of low-down, cowardly skunks trying to bushwhack me from the shadows."

Brinker's lips pulled back from his teeth in a grimace of hate. Controlling himself with a visible effort, he said, "You like to run that mouth of yours, don't you? But words don't mean nothin' compared to hot lead or cold steel."

"You're the one talking now."

"I'll do more than that, you—" Brinker's hand curled into a claw and hovered over the butt of his gun. Fargo was ready to move, to step away from the Ovaro and Spaulding and get them out of the line of fire in case Brinker started the ball. He didn't want to force a showdown just yet, but he would match his draw against Brinker's if he had to.

Again Brinker fought down the urge to kill. "Come on, boys," he said to his companions. "Let's go someplace where the air's better. That old man stinks."

Spaulding didn't seem bothered by the insult. He said, "On the contrary, my good man, I am a veritable bouquet of posies compared to the odiferous assault on the olfactory senses that is embodied in your personage."

One of Brinker's pards asked, "Did he just say *you* stink, Jed?"

Brinker growled and made a curt motion for the others to follow him as he stalked off along the boardwalk.

Fargo called after them, "I saw the dust you and your boys raised on the other side of the river coming out here, Brinker. I reckon once you got ahead of us, you must have split up and sent a few of your gunnies after the professor here while the rest of you raided that wagon train. And both bunches failed."

Brinker paused for a second, and again Fargo thought the head Coltman might go for his gun. But then with a little shake of his head Brinker went on. The others followed him, muttering to each other.

Spaulding asked worriedly, "Are you sure it was wise to reveal your suspicions to them, Mr. Fargo? If you're correct in your theories—and I feel certain that you are—they now know that you represent a threat to them."

"They already knew that, Professor," Fargo said. "Anyway, the way Brinker feels about me, I reckon I've had a target painted on my back ever since I left Missouri. What I hope is that by prodding Brinker, I can also push Coleman into taking action. That'll force him to come out into the open."

"Right where you want him, eh? I see the logic of your tactics now, and they have the potential to be very effective. But they're also dangerous, Mr. Fargo, quite dangerous."

"So's getting up in the morning," Fargo said with a smile. "Come on, Professor. I've got enough money to pay for a stall in the livery stable for this old boy, and then we'll mosey on down to that wagon of yours. It's been a long day."

7

Fargo recalled that Henry Coleman had mentioned owning the best livery stable in Topeka, so he found one that Coleman didn't own and paid the old man there to look after the Ovaro.

The liveryman said, "Folks around town have heard about how you stood up to Coleman, mister, and how you helped that preacher bring in those supplies. We're mighty beholden to you. I hate to take your money." He held out his hand with the coin that Fargo had given him lying on his palm.

Fargo closed the old-timer's callused hand over the coin. "You take it," he said. "Take good care of my horse and you'll have more than earned it."

"I'll take care of him, all right. You can count on that. I got an old scattergun in the office, and anybody who comes messin' around here is liable to get hisself a face full o' buckshot."

Fargo left his saddle at the livery stable but carried the Henry, his saddlebags, and his bedroll with him down to the professor's wagon.

"Home sweet home," Spaulding said. "Be it ever so humble."

"I'm surprised you're not staying in the hotel, Professor."

"Well, until I've earned my fee, economy is called

for. And I have no doubt that Coleman owns the best hostelry in town, so I wouldn't want to stay there anyway."

"I feel the same way," Fargo agreed with a grin. "The ground is a better mattress than any bed owned by Henry Coleman."

Spaulding got his bedroll from the wagon and spread it out on the ground underneath the vehicle. The wagon was large, providing plenty of room for Fargo's bedroll. He crawled into his blankets, tipped his hat down over his face, and with the true frontiersman's natural ability to fall asleep almost anywhere, he dozed off immediately.

He slept lightly—a part of his brain still alert for anything unusual going on around the wagon, any sign of a threat. Fargo didn't think Coleman and Brinker would try anything right here in the middle of town, at least not yet, but he wasn't going to take a chance on being wrong.

He awoke the next morning to the sound of a brass band, of all things. The musicians weren't particularly good—the notes were tinny and off-key—but what they lacked in skill they made up for with enthusiasm. The martial music had plenty of gusto.

Fargo rolled out of his blankets and was a little surprised to see that the sun was up and people were starting to move around the street. He didn't usually sleep that late. The professor stood beside the wagon, buttoning his high collar and tightening his tie.

"Good morning," Spaulding greeted him heartily. "I take it you slept well, Mr. Fargo?"

"Better than I expected to," Fargo admitted. "That sounds like a celebration getting under way."

"Yes, indeed. Today is the inaugural day of the Shawnee County Fair and Extravaganza."

"How long is it supposed to run?"

"The fair will conclude three days hence, with its culmination being a demonstration of my abilities."

"That's when you make it rain, eh?"

"Indeed."

Fargo pulled on his boots and put on his hat, then walked with the professor down the street. They came to a hash house and went inside to eat breakfast, but as they entered a man in an apron behind the counter held up his hands and said, "Sorry, boys. If you're lookin' for somethin' to eat, all I've got are a few eggs."

"Eggs will do fine," Fargo told him, "if they're fried up proper."

"What about coffee?" Spaulding asked.

The proprietor nodded. "I got coffee . . . for now."

"We're all set, then," Fargo said. He and Spaulding sat down at the counter. They were the only customers.

Somewhat apologetically, the owner said, "Uh, the price is gonna be a mite high. Not as high as what you'd be charged in Henry Coleman's restaurant, mind you, but still higher than I like."

Fargo nodded. "We understand. Supplies are scarce. Maybe that will change soon."

"Undoubtedly it will," Spaulding declared.

They ate two eggs each and drank two cups of coffee. Then they walked down to the Baptist church to check on the supply wagons. A crowd had already begun to gather, as people lined up for the supplies that would be distributed.

"Skye!"

Fargo turned around as he heard Sallie McCabe call his name.

"How are you this morning?" he greeted her.

"I'm fine," she said over the clamor of the townspeople. "I can tell we're going to have our hands full keeping order. Everyone is so anxious to get some supplies from the wagons. Sheriff Tucker promised to come by and help keep things under control."

"Well, if you need me, I'll be around," Fargo said. "Where's Reuben?"

"Right here," the big mountain man rumbled from behind Fargo. Fargo looked around and saw that Reuben was on his feet again, although he carried himself carefully and a little gingerly. Reuben had a sawed-off shotgun tucked under his left arm. The stock had been cut off, too, so that it served more as a pistol grip. It took a big, strong man to handle a weapon like that one-handed.

"You look like you're ready to go to war," Fargo commented with a smile.

"I'll be sittin' up on one of the wagons where I can keep an eye on things. If anybody gets too rambunctious, they'll have to deal with me and this ol' blunderbuss o' mine."

"With such an impressive sentinel standing watch, anyone would be a fool to cause a disturbance," Spaulding said.

The band was still playing, and people began to gather in front of the bandstand. Down the street, tables were carried out of the town hall and set up outside. Some of the ladies of the town brought out homemade quilts, along with other examples of fine needlework, and set them up for display on the tables. Farther along the street, a passel of pigs were driven into an empty corral. Later in the day the swine would be slathered with grease, and the boys of the town would be turned loose to see who could catch one first. As fairs went, it wasn't much, but to the long-suffering citizens of Topeka, any entertainment at all was a welcome relief.

Spaulding rubbed his hands together. "I must commence my activities now."

"I thought you weren't going to make it rain until the end of the fair," Fargo said.

"Very true, but one doesn't simply snap one's fingers and produce precipitation. The atmosphere must be properly prepared. Care to come along, Mr. Fargo?"

"Sure," Fargo said with a shrug. He didn't have anything better to do right this minute.

"Good. I could use a hand unloading some of my equipment."

"Going to put me to work, eh?" Fargo asked with a grin.

"All in a good cause, my young friend, all in a good cause."

They returned to Spaulding's wagon, where they unloaded several large pieces of equipment. Fargo thought one of the contraptions resembled a moonshine still, with its big cast-iron boiler and coils of copper tubing. Instead of leading down, the tubing led up to some sort of flared chamber with several pipes sticking up from the top of it.

There was also a piece that looked like a windmill blade lying on its side. It sat on top of a tripod of metal legs and had a crank attached to it. Fargo examined it closely but couldn't figure out what in the world it was for.

Another piece of equipment was in several sections. Fargo carried them out of the wagon, and Spaulding assembled the contraption. When completed, a vertical metal tube about six inches in diameter sat beside the wagon, braced on all four sides by metal legs that attached to a framework around the tube. The only piece left in the wagon was a large object covered by a sheet of canvas. Spaulding told Fargo to leave it alone for the time being.

"What is all this stuff, Professor?"

"Watch and learn, my boy, watch and learn."

Spaulding took some wood from a woodbox attached to the side of the wagon and opened a door in the bottom section of the boiler. In it he built a fire, then drew water from the public well to fill up the upper section.

"I always try to set up near a water supply for that very reason," he explained to Fargo. "That can be difficult in drought-stricken areas, of course, and that's usually where my services are needed. This well, however, seems to be in fairly good shape. If need be, we can bring water from the river. While it lacks a strong flow, it will be sufficient for my purposes."

With a slight frown, Fargo said, "Seems to me you're supposed to be bringing more water to these parts, not using what's already here."

"Despite appearances, rain is not created out of thin air, Mr. Fargo. There must be moisture in order for precipitation to form. Therefore, the atmosphere must be properly conditioned beforehand."

Soon the water in the boiler began to bubble. The steam was captured by a hood over the top of the boiler, and as it rose it was forced through the winding copper tube. Whistling softly to himself, the professor fetched a can of something from the wagon and dumped it into the boiler. Instantly the steam increased, taking on a faint yellowish tinge and giving off a smell like rotten eggs.

"Sulphur," Fargo guessed.

"Not exactly, although sulphur is one of the ingredients. It's a mixture of my own devising, and therefore the exact combination of elements is a secret. It's all part of properly conditioning the air for rain."

"Don't worry, Professor," Fargo said. "I don't intend to take up rainmaking, so I'm not going to steal your secrets."

The steam made its way through the tubing into the upper chamber. After a minute it began to rise from the pipes on top, which served as chimneys. Spaulding wasn't content to let the smoke climb into the sky at its own pace. He grasped the handle crank on the other machine and began to crank it. The metal blades that reminded Fargo of a windmill began to revolve slowly. They went faster and faster as Spaulding turned the crank, and the air current they created caught the smoke coming from the other contraption and lifted it higher and faster.

After a few minutes Spaulding began to grow red-faced from the effort. Fargo said, "Let me give you a hand with that, Professor."

"No need," Spaulding said. A crowd had gathered around the wagon and the odd-looking apparatus. Several adolescent boys watched wide-eyed, and Spaulding called out to one of them, "You, there, son! Would you like to help operate my atmosphere-conditioning machine, my boy?"

"Would I!" the youngster yelped in excitement. He hurried forward. "Sure! Just tell me what to do, Professor."

"Just keep turning this crank so that the blades revolve and the smoke from my special solution is carried high into the sky. Can you do that?"

"I sure can!" The boy grasped the crank as Spaulding released it and turned it with all the strength and enthusiasm of youth. The other boys in the crowd immediately clamored for their turn.

"Pretty slick, Professor," Fargo said quietly as Spaulding stepped back. "Those kids will be happy to do your work for you."

"The real work is in knowing how to prepare the solution and then activate the precipitation process once the atmosphere has been properly conditioned. That's how I earn my fee."

Fargo nodded. He wasn't convinced that Spaulding could really make it rain, not by a long shot. At least the professor seemed genuine in his belief that he could. He was an honest charlatan, if there could be such a thing.

Spaulding moved off to talk to the crowd and exhort them to a higher pitch of excitement, promising all sorts of wonders that would climax with a badly needed rainstorm. He worked the onlookers with all the skill and passion of a carnival pitchman.

"Quite a character, isn't he?"

Fargo looked over to see Diane Ainsley strolling up. She looked ravishing in a gray dress with white lace trim.

"Morning, Miss Ainsley. The professor seems to know what he's doing," Fargo said.

"You mean you think he'll really make it rain?"

"No, but he's got that crowd eating out of his hand, doesn't he?"

Diane frowned. "Do you mean he's a swindler, just out to take the town for money?"

"Not at all, but part of what he does is to entertain folks." Fargo kept his voice pitched low so that only Diane could hear him. "Look at their faces. Some of them believe that the professor can do what he says he can, while others don't believe it at all. But they're all interested. Even the ones who don't believe, in the back of their minds they're hoping that there'll turn out to be something to it."

"So what Professor Spaulding is really selling to them is optimism?"

Fargo nodded. "I would have said hope, but I reckon it's about the same thing."

Diane turned to Fargo and spoke seriously. "I'd like to talk to you, Mr. Fargo."

"I thought we were talking."

"No, I mean in private. An interview, I guess you could say. You're well known across the frontier. It's not every day that the Trailsman comes to Topeka."

Fargo's forehead creased slightly. "I didn't set out to be famous. And a lot of the things that have been written about me are just flat-out wrong."

"Well, then, an interview and an article in the *Clarion* would be your opportunity to set the record straight, now wouldn't it?"

Fargo couldn't argue—he hadn't realized that she was a journalist.

"All right," he said, "but only if you agree that I can buy you dinner."

"There's really not a good place in town to eat, unless you want to go to Coleman's restaurant."

"I'll pass on that," Fargo said. "And I'm willing to wait until after the drought breaks."

"Now you're the one being optimistic . . . but all right, that would be fine. Come over to the office with me?"

"Sure."

They walked down the street to the *Clarion* office. Fargo expected Thomas Ainsley to be there, but he didn't see any sign of him.

"Where's your brother?"

"He went to interview Mr. McCabe. There's going to be a lot of news for this week's edition, what with the county fair, the arrival of that wagon train, and you being in Topeka, Mr. Fargo."

"Call me Skye."

"It's usually not a good idea for a journalist to be too friendly with someone who's being interviewed.

But I suppose it wouldn't hurt anything in this case . . . Skye."

They sat down, Diane at one of the desks and Fargo straddling a ladder-back chair nearby. She pulled over a pad of paper and a pencil and asked him questions about his life, the places he had been and the things he had done. He deflected the questions about his early years—he didn't ever talk much about that time in his life—and tried to be as honest as he could about the rest. Diane had to write quickly just to keep up with him.

She glanced up and pushed back a strand of midnight black hair that had fallen over her face. "You've led an incredibly eventful existence, Skye. How did you manage to pack so much into such a short span of years?"

"I've never liked to let the grass grow under my feet," Fargo replied with a smile.

"This is going to make an excellent story. Thank you, Skye."

"It was my pleasure," Fargo told her. "You're just about the prettiest reporter I've ever talked to."

She smiled back at him. "Do you make a habit of flirting with the journalists who interview you?"

"Well, considering the fact that most of 'em have muttonchop whiskers and smoke vile cigars . . . no, not hardly."

Diane laughed. "I think I'm looking forward to that dinner with you."

"I know I am." Fargo got to his feet. "Right now, though, I reckon I'll head back down to the church and see how things are going there. Anything you want me to tell your brother if I run into him?"

"No, I can't think of anything. He should be back soon."

Fargo nodded and left the newspaper office. He liked Diane Ainsley, and not just because she was so pretty. She was smart and independent, and Fargo thought highly of those qualities in a woman.

The brass band was still playing, but they seemed to be losing steam and weren't playing with the enthusiasm that they had earlier. The biggest crowd was at the Baptist church. Fargo headed in that direction.

He had gone a block when a muffled cry caught his attention as he was passing the mouth of an alley. He looked along the narrow, shadowy space and saw a flash of movement at the far end. A second later he heard the unmistakable sound of fists thudding against flesh. Fargo hesitated only a second before striding quickly along the alley. This might not be any of his business, but he wasn't the sort who could stand idly by while someone was in trouble.

Suddenly a man staggered around the rear corner of one of the buildings. His face was bloody.

A bigger man lunged around the corner after him, grabbing him by the collar and flinging him against the wall. Two more appeared. All were hard-featured and roughly dressed. The big man drew back a booted foot and growled, "All right, boys, let's kick the hell out of him."

Fargo said, "I don't reckon that would be a very good idea."

His voice carried clearly down the alley, and the men froze. Music still hung tinnily in the distance. The three men stared at Fargo, and he instantly recognized them as members of the gun crew headed by Jed Brinker.

"Fargo!" one of them spat.

"Let's ventilate him!" snarled another.

"No!" the first man ordered. "Jed wants that one for himself." To Fargo he continued, "Back off, mister. This is none of your business."

"I'm making it my business," Fargo said as he stepped slowly down the alley toward them. His eyes darted down at the injured man's face—he had recognized Thomas Ainsley. The newspaperman lay sprawled in the dust, moaning. He seemed to be only half-conscious.

"You're makin' a big mistake, Fargo," the first hardcase warned him.

"Wouldn't be the first time," Fargo replied coolly. His hand was close to the butt of his Colt, just in case the gunmen decided to slap leather.

"Jed said not to kill Fargo if we ran into him," mused one of the other men, "but he didn't say anything about not beatin' the hell out of him, did he?"

"No," the first man agreed. "He didn't say that at all."

And with that he lunged at Fargo, swinging a wild punch.

Fargo just barely ducked under the blow. He stepped in and slammed a quick right and left to the man's midsection that sent him gasping and reeling against the wall. The other two were right behind him—Fargo couldn't avoid both of them. One of them tagged him with a solid punch that rocked his head back, sending his hat flying. Fargo caught himself on his back foot, swayed forward, and smashed a fist into the face of his nearest attacker.

The second man hooked a punch to the kidneys that made Fargo gasp in pain. He fought it off, drove an elbow into the man's solar plexus, and then looped a punch to the side of his head. The man went down.

The other two were still on their feet and still in the fight. They came at Fargo from the sides. Using all the speed he could summon, he grabbed the man on his right by the shirtfront, pivoted and swayed backward at the same time, hauling the man forward so that he crashed head-on into his companion. Their skulls came together with a solid *clunk!* They staggered back a few steps, and then collapsed, knocked silly by their collision.

Breathing hard from the exertion of the brief but intense fight, Fargo retrieved his hat, then bent down and grasped Thomas Ainsley under the arms.

"Come on," Fargo said to the newspaperman, pulling him to his feet. "Let's get you back to your office."

"F-Fargo? . . ." Ainsley said.

"That's right." Fargo glanced over Ainsley's body— the man didn't have any gunshot or knife wounds. His face was bloody from a few cuts, his lip and one eye were swollen, and bruises were starting to form on his jaw. Other than being on the receiving end of a beating, Ainsley was probably all right.

They reached the end of the alley and Fargo helped Ainsley step awkwardly up onto the boardwalk. From behind him he heard Sheriff Avery Tucker call out, "What the hell!"

Fargo looked back over his shoulder at the lawman hurrying toward him. He jerked his head toward the alley and said, "There are three men down there who jumped Ainsley and gave him a beating."

Tucker stared at Fargo. "You kill 'em?"

"Nope, they're just knocked out. You might want to get your deputies and haul them off to jail."

"That's just what I'll do, by gum," Tucker said grimly. He drew his revolver and headed down the alley.

Fargo helped Ainsley along the boardwalk to the *Clarion* office. Diane looked up from her desk as they limped in and let out a startled cry. "Oh, my God! Tom!" She leaped up and rushed over. "What happened to him? Is he all right?"

Ainsley's senses were returning to him. "I . . . I'm

not hurt too bad, Diane," he managed to say. "They just . . . walloped me a few times."

"Who did this?" Diane demanded, and at that moment her dark blue eyes were filled with righteous fury.

"Three of Brinker's men," Fargo replied, "which means they really work for Coleman, I reckon."

Ainsley nodded weakly as Fargo eased him down into a chair. "Yes, you can be sure that Coleman was behind this attack. Brinker may have passed along the orders, but Coleman gave them to start with."

"Coleman must really hate you."

"I've been using the *Clarion* to fight against the way he's been gradually taking over the entire county. Coleman has done everything in his power to get back at me legally." Ainsley gave a humorless laugh. "I guess he decided since that hasn't shut me up, he'd take a more direct track."

"We won't let him get away with this," Diane said hotly. "We'll have the law on him now."

Fargo pointed out, "There probably won't be anything to link Coleman directly with what happened. Those men who jumped your brother will likely claim it was their own idea and insist that Coleman didn't have anything to do with it. Again, it's a matter of knowing the truth but not being able to prove it."

"The hell with proof!" Diane blazed.

Ainsley caught hold of her hand. "You don't mean that," he said. "If we take the law into our own hands, we're no better than he is, Diane."

Fargo didn't say anything. Those were noble sentiments Ainsley expressed, and there were plenty of times when he would have been right.

But there were other times on the frontier when the only law that truly existed was what a man held in his own hands. Sometimes there was no other answer, and when evil grew up like the grass, it was up to good men to chop it back down.

Hopefully, things hadn't gotten to that point in Topeka. Sheriff Tucker would do what he could to see that justice was served, and Fargo would do his part to help out.

"I've got an idea about getting the proof we need," he said to Ainsley and Diane. "Just hold on a mite longer and maybe we'll put Coleman out of business permanently."

"What are you talking about, Skye?" Diane asked.

"I'll let you know when I'm sure about it. Until then, you'd better have a doctor take a look at you, Tom."

Ainsley waved off that suggestion. "I'm fine," he insisted. "I've got to get to work. The stories for the next edition won't write themselves."

He struggled to stand, then dropped back down heavily as a wave of dizziness went through him.

"I'm going for the doctor," Diane insisted. "Skye, will you stay here and keep an eye on this stubborn brother of mine?"

"Sure," Fargo replied.

Diane hurried out. Ainsley sat, elbows on the table, with his aching head in his hands. "There's no arguing with my sister," he said dully.

"No, I imagine not," Fargo agreed. Diane Ainsley was definitely feisty.

That was another thing he liked in a woman.

8

Diane returned a few minutes later with the doctor. The sawbones cleaned the blood from Ainsley's face, and carefully stitched up the deepest gash while Ainsley sat stoically. When finished, the doctor declared that what the newspaperman needed more than anything else was some rest.

"That'll have to wait," Ainsley declared. "I have too much to do."

The doctor snapped his black bag closed. "That's up to you," he said. "Don't blame me, though, when you pass out."

"He'll rest," Diane said grimly. "I'll see to that."

Fargo slipped out of the newspaper office, not interested in listening to the argument between the two siblings. He walked across the street and down a couple of blocks to the jail. The brass band had finally given up and called a halt to the concert.

Sheriff Tucker had Ainsley's attackers behind bars. "They claim Tom Ainsley insulted 'em, and that's why they jumped him," the lawman told Fargo.

Fargo nodded as he perched a hip on the corner of Tucker's desk. "I'm not surprised. That's about what I expected from them. To hear them tell it, Brinker and Coleman didn't have a thing to do with what happened, did they?"

"Nary a blessed thing." Tucker sighed. "They might

change their tune if I whaled on 'em for a while with a two-by-four."

"Don't do that," Fargo said with a shake of his head. "I hope to have something better on Coleman soon."

"Care to let me in on it, son?"

"Not just yet," Fargo said.

Tucker grunted. "Play your cards mighty close to the vest, don't you?"

"That way nobody can see what I'm holding," Fargo replied with a smile.

He left the sheriff's office and headed for the church.

He saw that the crowd was smaller than before. Joshua McCabe strolled over and said, "Hello, Mr. Fargo."

"Looks like things have settled down a bit."

McCabe nodded. "Yes, they have, and I'm glad. People have proven to be pretty reasonable. We're rationing out the supplies very strictly, to make them go as far as possible and help as many people as we can. A few folks have argued and wanted more, but not many."

Fargo inclined his head toward the wagon where Reuben Sanborn sat watching over the distribution of supplies. "I imagine Reuben's had something to do with that. Nobody with any sense wants a gent like him mad at them."

McCabe frowned. "I'm glad you mentioned Reuben, Mr. Fargo. He seems like a good man, but . . . well, he and Sallie are getting pretty fond of each other, and I want to make sure he's not going to do anything to hurt her. Sallie's young, and mighty innocent."

Remembering what had happened between him and Sallie McCabe in Missouri, Fargo figured that "innocent" wasn't one of the words he would use to describe her. But he knew what McCabe meant, and he said reassuringly, "You don't have to worry about Reuben. He looks and sounds a little like a grizzly bear, but he's a good man and honest as the day is long."

"Yes, but is he the sort to lead a girl on and then abandon her? He doesn't seem like the kind of man who would want to settle down."

"You'd be surprised," Fargo said. "When I first ran into him this time, he was talking about doing just that."

"Well, I guess all I can do is wait and see what happens. Sallie's got a mind of her own, you know. If I try to tell her what to do, that's the quickest way to get her to do just the opposite."

"She's a smart girl," Fargo told the preacher. "She'll be fine."

He watched as Sallie climbed onto the wagon next to Reuben and spoke in a quiet, intimate voice, sharing something that was only between the two of them. Reuben laughed, and Sallie smiled at him.

Fargo felt a little pang of regret that he wasn't on the receiving end of that smile, and likely wouldn't ever get any more like that from Sallie McCabe. But the feeling passed quickly, replaced by one of happiness for Sallie and Reuben. What Fargo had missed in his life as far as simple domestic pleasures went had been more than adequately replaced by the things he had seen and the adventures he had experienced.

Fargo strolled back up the street toward Professor Spaulding's wagon. The rainmaker still had a crowd gathered around him. A different youngster was turning the crank on the wind machine as the boiler spewed steam. Spaulding stood by watching in satisfaction with his thumbs hooked in his vest.

"How's the air?" Fargo asked him. "Getting ready to rain?"

"In due time, my friend, in due time." The professor rocked back and forth on his feet and squinted at the cloudless sky. The steam dissipated as quickly as it rose. "Everything may seem high and dry to you," he went on, "but to an experienced eye such as mine, the heavens are simply ripe with the possibility of precipitation."

"I'll take your word for it. That just looks like a pretty blue sky to me. Must be hard to work your cloud wizardry when there's no clouds."

"Patience, my boy. Patience is everything in this game."

Fargo moved on, passing the women looking over the display of colorful quilts. He cast a glance at the Grand Kansas Saloon and considered going in for a drink. Coleman would have heard by now about his men getting arrested for their attack on Thomas Ainsley. The saloonkeeper was probably seething with anger at having his plans thwarted. He struck Fargo as the sort who didn't like to be crossed by anybody.

Fargo's plan was to goad Coleman into doing something foolish, but he wasn't quite ready to do that just yet. Better to wait a while, he decided. Like the sulphurous concoction bubbling away in Professor Spaulding's rainmaking contraption, Fargo would let the situation in Topeka boil a little longer and get a little hotter.

The day passed peacefully enough. More families came into town from the surrounding farms, eager to take in the sights and sounds of the county fair. The band played again in the afternoon and drew quite a crowd.

Fargo circulated, moving from one end of the street

to the other and back again, keeping an eye out for signs of trouble. Brinker and his bunch seemed to be lying low. He didn't see them anywhere and supposed they were in the Grand Kansas Saloon. Between the men who were now in jail and the ones he had wounded or killed during the raid on the wagon train, he figured he had done some significant damage to the gang.

Late in the afternoon, hearing some sort of commotion from the area around Professor Spaulding's wagon, Fargo headed in that direction and arrived in time to see the rainmaker loading a four-foot-long cylinder into the vertical tube he had set up earlier. Fargo realized what it was even before Spaulding lit the fuse and sent the rocket hurtling straight up into the sky. The crowd gasped in awe.

Fargo watched the rocket climb, trailing sparks and smoke from its base as the lifting charge burned. When it was high overhead it burst in a brilliant explosion. That brought cheers from the crowd.

Spaulding was busy adjusting the launching tube so that the next rocket would ascend at an angle and thus carry into a different part of the sky. He paused just long enough to nod at Fargo.

"Fireworks, Professor?" Fargo asked.

"Pyrotechnical diffusion of precipitation-inducing elements," Spaulding explained. "Now that the conditioning of the air has properly begun, it's time to add condensate matter."

"If you say so," Fargo replied with a shake of his head. "Those rockets blow up real pretty, too. Folks like to watch that."

"Indeed they do," the professor agreed. He had the next rocket ready to go. He touched it off, and again the narrow tube climbed high in the sky on a tail of flame before bursting in an impressive shower of light.

Spaulding continued firing rockets as dusk settled down over Topeka and the surrounding prairie. Finally he announced that that was all for today, adding that the rainmaking exhibition would resume the following morning. The crowd was disappointed, but several fiddle players had started sawing away down the street, and folks were already starting to dance. The people around Spaulding's wagon drifted away.

"Do you plan to leave this gear out tonight, Professor?" Fargo asked.

"Certainly. It's too heavy to steal easily, and besides, no one would have a real reason to bother it."

"What about Coleman and Brinker?"

Spaulding frowned. "That's right. I had forgotten about those two misbegotten miscreants. I suppose I shall have to stand guard all night . . . unless I could prevail upon you, Mr. Fargo . . ."

"Maybe later," Fargo said. "I've got something else I need to do first, though."

"Something to do with the fair Miss Ainsley, I'd wager?"

Fargo grunted. "I wish that was true, Professor. What I have in mind won't be anywhere near as pleasant, I'm afraid."

He went back to the restaurant where he and Spaulding had eaten breakfast and found that the proprietor had slaughtered a pig during the day. After a light supper of pork and fried eggs, Fargo stepped outside into a dark night. He looked along the street and noticed lights burning at the *Clarion* office. He thought again about Diane Ainsley and how attractive she was.

Beauty had to wait. Fargo walked the other way, toward the dark, looming hulks of the warehouses where Henry Coleman hoarded the supplies he sold for such exorbitant prices.

The warehouses fronted on the main street, sitting side by side like a pair of great beasts. Fargo headed for the rear of the closest one, cat-footing through the shadows alongside the building.

When he reached the back he slipped along the wall, looking for some way in. He found it in a narrow door that was locked. Fargo slid his Arkansas Toothpick from its sheath on his leg and probed with the tip of the blade. He worked it into the narrow crack between the door and the jamb and then leaned his weight against the knife, forcing the blade in farther. It took several minutes of prying back and forth, but the door, while sturdily built, wasn't meant to stand up to that. The lock sprung, and the door sagged open a couple of inches.

Fargo's actions had been almost soundless. Carefully, he eased the door open, careful not to let the hinges squeak. When the door was just far enough ajar, he slipped into the darkened interior. He pulled the door behind him, leaving a gap of less than an inch.

For a long moment he stood there, silent and motionless, letting his keen senses reach out. The place was not completely dark. A little light from the moon and stars came in through the tiny gap around the door, and that was enough for Fargo's eyes. He could tell that he was in some sort of small office at the back of the warehouse. He moved carefully across the room and found a door. It wasn't locked.

This door opened into the big, cavernous chamber of the warehouse itself. A lantern hung from a suspended rope, and the reflected glow revealed stacks of crates and barrels with narrow aisles running crookedly between them. Fargo stepped out of the office, using the old Indian trick of putting the ball of his foot down first before letting the rest of his weight down. With all the stealth he could muster, he worked his way toward the front of the building.

He heard two men talking. One of them let out a laugh. As he came closer, he heard the soft slapping sound of cards being shuffled and dealt. The guards were passing the time with a game.

Fargo knew it might take him a while to find what he was looking for, if he could even find it at all. Therefore he had to deal with the guards, so that he could work uninterrupted. He put his foot against one of the crates and shoved it, not much but enough to move it an inch or so. The wood rasped against the floor.

"What the hell was that?" exclaimed one of the guards.

"Just a rat, more'n likely," the other man said. "You in or out? The bet's four bits to you."

"Hang on, damn it. That sounded like somebody moved one of those boxes. A rat couldn't do that."

"No, but a rat could drag a piece of broken board across the floor. That's what it sounded like to me. Are you playin' or not?"

"Yeah, damn it, I guess I am."

Fargo heard the jingle of coins as they dropped onto the table.

"I don't much like that, though. Coleman will have our hides if anything happens to any of this stuff."

"You mean he'll have Brinker get our hides," the other man said.

"We wind up without our hides either way," the first man pointed out. "That don't sound too pleasant to me."

"Well, then, go take a look around if you want."

"You think so?"

The second man snorted. "That's better than just sittin' there bitchin' and worryin', ain't it?"

"Yeah, you're right. I reckon we can finish this hand first, though."

That took only a moment. One of the guards laughed in triumph while the other man muttered a curse. Then footsteps came toward Fargo's position.

"I'll be right back."

"Yell if you see anything."

Fargo smiled thinly in the shadows as he heard that exchange between the guards. He didn't plan on anybody doing any yelling.

He drew back into a dark, narrow gap between two stacks of crates and eased his Colt out of its holster. The footsteps came closer as Fargo reversed the gun and held it by its barrel.

"See anything?"

"Not a blasted thing."

"It was a rat, I tell you."

The footsteps stopped. "Yeah, maybe you're right."

Fargo held his breath. He didn't want the searching guard to give up now. He slid a foot along the floor, making a tiny scraping noise.

"No, there's something here," the guard said as he came closer.

A moment later, he stepped past the little alcove where Fargo waited. Fargo struck with the speed and deadly accuracy of a snake, smashing the butt of his gun down on the guard's head. The man's hat softened the blow a little and muffled the sound of it thudding home. Fargo reached out with his other hand and grabbed the shotgun that the guard held before the man could drop it. The unconscious guard slumped to the floor, landing with a dull thud.

"Ted? Ted, did you find something?"

Fargo laid the shotgun carefully on the floor. He bent down and grasped the fallen man under the arms, then hauled him into the shadows. The man's boots scraped against the floor.

"Ted, damn it, answer me!"

Fargo ducked behind a barrel as he heard a rush of footsteps. His plan seemed to be working, but if the second guard ran for help instead of investigating the sudden disappearance of his friend, Fargo would have to slip out the back of the warehouse and try again later.

Luckily, the guard's curiosity got the best of him, and he stepped closer. For the second time Fargo's Colt rose and fell, and the butt of the gun thudded down on the back of an unwary guard's head. He fell to his knees but didn't pass out right away. His scattergun lifted to bear on the Trailsman.

Fargo kicked the weapon aside, and looped a punch into the guard's face. The blow landed solidly, stunning the man and knocking him flat on his back. Fargo bent over him, jerked the man's belt off, rolled him over, and used the belt to lash his hands together behind his back. He stuffed the guard's sweaty bandanna into his mouth.

Fargo did the same with the first man, then found some rope and tied their feet as well.

With the guards out of the way, Fargo got to work on the task that had brought him here. A lantern sat on a barrel beside the crate where a deck of greasy cards were scattered. The guards had been using two more crates as chairs. Fargo lifted the lantern from the barrel and began his search.

He checked the office first, but found nothing of interest. He hadn't expected that he would. Coleman was too careful for that. Fargo began examining every crate and barrel in the warehouse.

After a while he heard some muffled sounds and a

few thumps. One or both of the gagged, hog-tied guards had regained consciousness, but they couldn't do anything about the predicament in which they found themselves.

Fargo's frustration grew as he searched. Some of the crates bore labels giving the names and addresses of the companies they had come from. He could use that information to trace the original buyer, but that would prove a costly and time-consuming process. He hoped to find something that would settle the question quicker.

Finally, he spotted a piece of paper sticking out from under one of the crates. He bent to grasp it, putting his shoulder against the crate and heaving up. With his fingers he slipped the scrap of paper free.

He held it in the light of the lantern. The paper was raggedly torn, but enough of it remained to see that it was part of a bill of lading. Most of the area that showed to whom the freight had been consigned had been ripped off, but a small piece remained. Fargo saw the letters "—yson Frei—" and part of a Topeka address.

That was it, he thought as he stared down at the scrap of paper, the proof he needed. These goods had been consigned to the Tyson Freight Company, which had been owned by the late Walt Tyson. And yet here they sat in Henry Coleman's warehouse. The only way they could have gotten here was if Jed Brinker and his gunmen had stolen them from one of Tyson's wagons, before Tyson had been murdered to get him out of the way.

Possession of stolen property wasn't nearly as serious a crime as murder, of course, but it would be enough for Sheriff Tucker to arrest Coleman. That was the first step in breaking the iron grip Coleman had on the citizens of Topeka. Fargo didn't know how Brinker would react when his boss was thrown in jail. Chances were, that would bust things wide open.

Fargo would be ready to deal with Brinker's threat if that happened.

For now, though, he had to get this evidence to the sheriff. They would decide how to proceed from there.

He avoided the trussed-up guards as he left the warehouse. Neither of them had been able to get a good look at him. He had moved too fast and the interior of the warehouse was too shadowy. Fargo wanted to keep it that way. No doubt the guards would be discovered in the morning, if not sooner, and although Coleman would know that someone had invaded the warehouse, he wouldn't have any way of knowing who or why. The fact that none of the supplies had been stolen would probably puzzle him.

He wouldn't be puzzled for long, Fargo thought. He wasn't sure when the best time would be for the law to make its move against Coleman, but it was bound to be soon.

Topeka couldn't stand much of a delay.

A light burned in the sheriff's office. Fargo went in and found Tucker at his desk.

"Take a look at that," Fargo said as he placed the scrap of paper in front of Tucker.

The sheriff leaned forward and squinted at the paper. "What is it?"

"That's part of a bill of lading consigning goods to the Tyson Freight Company." Fargo pointed out the remaining letters. "Walt Tyson never delivered those crates to Topeka, though."

"Where are they?" Tucker asked.

"Right now they're sitting in one of Henry Coleman's warehouses."

The sheriff looked up at Fargo, his eyes widening in realization of what that bit of news meant, and then he slapped a callused palm down on the desk.

"By Godfrey, we got him!" Tucker exclaimed. "I asked you for proof that Coleman had broke the law, and blamed if that ain't it, Fargo!"

"Is it enough to justify locking him up?"

Tucker reached for his hat. "It damn sure is! You want to come with me?"

Fargo held up a hand. He had done a lot of thinking on the way over here. "Hold on, Sheriff," he said. "I'm not sure if you want to arrest Coleman right away or not."

"Why not?" Tucker asked with a frown.

"The fair has two more days to run," Fargo said. "Coleman's arrest is going to cause a big uproar, more than likely. Brinker and his men will probably try to break him out of jail, and if that happens while a lot of people are in town, the chances are better that innocent people will be hurt. Why not wait until the fair is over and then make your move against Coleman?"

Tucker's frown deepened. "I hate to see that son of a bitch get away with it for even an hour longer . . . but what you say makes sense, Fargo. I reckon it would be better to wait. But I still don't like it."

"Neither do I, Sheriff, but it'll be worth it when Coleman is behind bars."

"You really think Brinker will blow the town wide open?" Tucker asked worriedly.

"I think there's a good chance of it. But we'll be prepared for trouble by then. I'll pass the word to Tom Ainsley and to Joshua McCabe, and we'll have men armed and ready in case of a fight."

Tucker sighed. "What you're talkin' about is a small-scale war, Fargo."

The Trailsman nodded. "I reckon you're right, Sheriff . . . and it's a war we can't afford to lose."

The *Clarion* office was lit up, too, when Fargo stopped there a short time later. He heard the clatter of the printing press before he opened the door and stepped inside.

Tom and Diane Ainsley were both working at the big cumbersome machine. Their hands and aprons were smeared with ink. Diane even had a little smudge of ink on her chin, Fargo saw as she turned to look at him. He thought it made her even cuter.

Ainsley gestured for him to wait, and within a few minutes he and Diane stopped turning the cranks that ran the machine, and the noise died down. They turned to Fargo, and Ainsley asked, "What is it, Mr. Fargo? Is there more trouble?"

Fargo shook his head. "Nope. In fact, maybe it's the beginning of the end of Topeka's troubles."

Quickly, he filled them in on what he had found in Coleman's warehouse. Both of them grasped the implications immediately.

"This is just what we've been needing," Ainsley said.

"You've accomplished a great deal in the short time you've been here, Skye," Diane added.

"It's still a long way from over," Fargo pointed out. "The sheriff can arrest Coleman now, but that won't break the back of his power. He still has Brinker and those other gunmen working for him."

"But with Coleman in jail, he can't pay them," Ainsley said. "They'll have to try to get him out. In order to do that, they'll have to break the law themselves, and they can be arrested."

Fargo thought it unlikely that Jed Brinker and the

other hired guns would allow themselves to be thrown in jail. They would put up a fight.

"Just in case, you need to start passing the word to men you can trust," Fargo said. "Tell them there may be trouble and to be ready for it. Don't say anything to anybody unless you know they're dependable, though. We don't want Coleman getting wind of this."

"No, of course not," Ainsley agreed.

"You look pretty worn out," Fargo commented. "The doctor said you ought to get some rest after being roughed up like that."

Ainsley waved that off. "I'm fine. I'm just tired, and I do have a bit of a headache."

"I tried to get him to go to bed," Diane said, "but he insisted on helping me print these flyers for Professor Spaulding."

Fargo picked up one of the still slightly damp flyers that had come from the printing press. In big letters it advertised the professor's rainmaking show.

"If he can really make it rain, he'll go a long way toward putting Coleman out of business all by himself," Fargo said with a smile.

"I'm not sure I believe in rainmaking," Ainsley said. "The professor claims it's all scientific, but it's not like any science I ever heard of. He might as well be doing some sort of Indian rain dance."

"I've seen some of those work, too," Fargo said. "I reckon we'll just have to wait and see what happens."

9

Fargo was surprised to see a few clouds in the sky when he woke up the next morning. Maybe there was something to Professor Spaulding's talk about "conditioning" the air after all. The professor seemed quite pleased when he surveyed the heavens.

"Good progress," he told Fargo. "Good progress indeed. By tomorrow night, everything will be ready."

Fargo saw Sheriff Tucker later in the morning. With a grin, the lawman said, "Coleman came to see me first thing today. Claimed somebody broke into one o' his warehouses last night and assaulted two of his guards. He said it was my duty to find the culprits, as he called 'em. He admitted nothin' was stolen, though, and when I offered to go over and have a look around inside the warehouse, he changed his tune suddenlike. Guess he was so mad he wasn't thinkin' straight at first, but then he decided he didn't want the law pokin' around over there after all."

"Of course not," Fargo agreed. "He was afraid you might find more than he bargained for."

Topeka was even more crowded today, on the second day of the fair. The way things were going, just about everybody in the county would show up on the final day, especially since that was when Professor Spaulding was going to make it rain.

Both Sheriff Tucker and Tom Ainsley had spoken

122

to some of the townsmen and let them know that a move against Henry Coleman and his gang was coming up. Fargo talked to some of the men himself, warning them that they could expect trouble and making sure they knew to keep their mouths shut. He discussed the situation with Joshua McCabe and Reuben Sanborn as well.

"Count me in on any fight, Skye," Reuben declared. "I'm feelin' a lot better these days, like I could lick my weight in wildcats. I reckon a lot of that is because of the way Sallie's taken care of me."

"My daughter does seem to be devoted to you, Brother Sanborn," McCabe commented.

Reuben ran his fingers through his bushy black beard. "Well, now, Reverend, I've been meanin' to talk to you about Sallie. She's just about the finest gal I ever saw, and . . . and I'd be honored if you'd give me permission to seek her hand in marriage."

McCabe looked intently at Reuben for a long moment before answering. "You have my permission, Reuben. Remember, though, if you ever do anything to hurt that little girl, I can make that bullwhip of mine do some terrible things to a man's hide."

"I won't forget that, sir," Reuben said, "but you don't have to worry about me hurtin' Sallie. I'd sooner die first."

"All right, then. I won't say anything to her. You can ask her whenever you think it's the right time."

"Thank you, sir."

A few minutes later, when Fargo and Reuben were alone, the Trailsman chuckled. "I don't think you were that nervous the time you had to wrestle that grizzly, Reuben."

"Yeah, well, you try askin' a fella if you can marry his daughter and see how nervous you are," Reuben said as he wiped sweat off his forehead.

"No thanks," Fargo replied with a grin. "But if you think that was bad, just wait until it's time to ask Sallie herself."

Reuben just glared at him.

Fargo spent the rest of the day hanging around the professor's wagon and listening to the band play. A peaceful lull had come over Topeka. Despite the drought, despite the hard times that had gripped the area for the past eighteen months, people seemed to be having a genuinely good time at the fair. Fargo heard a lot of laughter, saw plenty of smiles.

Not from Brinker's gunmen, though. They lounged on the boardwalk in front of Coleman's saloon and glared at the festivities around them. The citizens of Topeka and the surrounding area had a little bit of hope again, and that was bad for Coleman's plans.

The professor was working harder than ever, firing off rockets and generating steam and exhorting the crowd. He built a big fire in an iron brazier and tossed handfuls of powder into the flames that sent brilliantly colored smoke climbing into the sky. Just getting all the proper elements in place, he explained to Fargo.

Late in the afternoon Fargo walked over to the newspaper office. Although Ainsley's bruises were almost as colorful as the smoke from the professor's little bonfire, he seemed to be recovered for the most part from the beating he had suffered the day before. He said to Fargo, "I wish you'd take Diane out of here and show her the sights of the fair. She never takes the time to get any enjoyment out of life."

"Well neither do you," she said to her brother. "You just work all the time, and I follow your example."

"You don't want to do that," Ainsley said with a laugh. "Go with Mr. Fargo. That's an order from your editor."

Fargo offered her his arm. "I'd be glad to attend the fair with you, ma'am."

Diane laughed and shook her head. "Oh, all right. I can see I'm wasting my time arguing with you two."

The fiddle players were back in business this evening. A big crowd had gathered to dance. It didn't take much persuasion on Fargo's part to get Diane to dance with him. Fargo loved the feel of her in his arms as they twirled around and around in time to the merry scrapings of the fiddlers.

Suddenly, Fargo heard a loud explosion. The booming report made the musicians quit playing, and all the dancers stopped in their tracks and swung around to see what had happened. A couple of women cried out in fear, and men shouted questions and curses as another, fainter blast sounded.

"Not to worry, my friends, not to worry!" The words came from Professor Spaulding. "Merely more preparations for the great rainmaking extravaganza tomorrow night!"

As Fargo strode toward the professor with Diane beside him, he saw Spaulding standing next to a cannon. That was the big thing that had been hidden under canvas inside the wagon, Fargo realized. The cannon's barrel had been cranked up to such an elevation that its charge had been fired high into the sky.

"Damn it, Professor, when you shoot a cannonball into the air, it's got to come down somewhere!" Fargo said. "There's no telling where it landed, or who it landed on."

"Never fear, my young friend," Spaulding said. "That was not a regular cannonball which I just launched into the heavens. It was equipped with a charge that detonated at the apogee of its ascent, thereby dispersing even more of the necessary particulate matter into the clouds."

One of the bystanders said, "You mean you shoot cannonballs at the clouds to make it rain, Professor?"

"To put it in the simplest of terms . . . yes."

The townsman nodded sagely. "Well, I reckon that makes sense."

Fargo didn't know if it did or not, but he didn't really care about that part of it. He said, "Be mighty careful with that cannon, Professor. There are a lot of people in town. You don't want it going off by accident."

"I assure you, Mr. Fargo, I have years of experience at this."

When the excitement died down, the fiddlers began playing again. Fargo and Diane went back to the dance.

When it was over they walked back toward the newspaper office arm in arm. He felt the soft warmth of her breast as she leaned against his side. When they reached the office they found it dark, and Diane said, "I guess Tom turned in early. That's not like him, but he needed the rest, I'm sure."

Fargo went inside with her. Instead of lighting a lamp as he expected her to, she turned toward him and moved even closer, sliding her arms around his neck. Fargo put his arms around her waist as she tipped her head back. He brought his mouth down on hers in a hot, searching kiss.

Her lips parted under the gentle prodding of his tongue. He explored the warm, wet cavern of her mouth, relishing the sweetness of her kiss. Her breasts flattened against his broad, muscular chest, and her pelvis molded against him. He was erect already. She groaned softly, deep in her throat, as she pressed herself against his hardness.

"I want you, Skye," she whispered when they finally

broke the kiss. "I know it's not proper to behave this way when I plan to write about you, but I can't help it." She reached down and caressed his manhood through the buckskin trousers. "I've wanted you ever since the first time I saw you."

"I feel the same way," Fargo told her, "but what about your brother? He's asleep right back there...."

"Tom is the heaviest sleeper in the world. He won't hear a thing . . . well, not if we don't make too much noise, that is. I know that from experience," she added mischievously.

"We'll see about that," Fargo promised. He scooped her up in his arms and carried her down the hall to the living quarters and into her bedroom.

They undressed each other in the dark. The only illumination in the room was the faint glow of light from the moon and stars that filtered through the gauzy curtains over the window. That was enough to make Diane's skin shine like pale silver as she stood nude before Fargo.

His eyes drank in the beautiful sight of her slender body. His gaze played over the high, firm breasts with their small brown nipples, the flat plane of her belly, the elegant flare of her hips, the rounded thighs, and the triangle of finespun black hair at the juncture of those thighs.

She was as beautiful a woman as he had seen in a long time. She seemed to appreciate his muscular, powerful body, too. Moving closer to him, she ran her hands over his chest, his shoulders, and his arms. He was fully erect, and Diane stood close enough to him so that the head of his engorged manhood pressed against the softness of her belly. She slid her hands down over his stomach and wrapped both of them around his long, thick shaft.

"You're magnificent, Skye," she whispered.

He reached out for her and she came willingly into his arms.

They kissed again, long and hungrily, and as they did Fargo cupped one of her breasts and stroked the pebbled nipple with his thumb. Diane reached around him and kneaded his muscular buttocks. She thrust her groin against his hardness, teasing the sensitive flesh with her lightly furred mound.

Fargo moved her back slowly until they reached the bed. Diane lay back on it, her legs parting naturally as she opened herself to him. Fargo moved between them, poised between her widespread thighs, and lowered his head to her femininity. Using his thumbs, he parted the folds of her sex and ran the tip of his tongue along the opening before sliding it into her. Her hips began to bob up and down on the bed, threatening to dislodge his lips and tongue as he licked and sucked and probed. The oral caresses lifted her higher and higher on a plateau of arousal.

Suddenly her thighs clamped shut on his head as her hips bucked wildly. Spasms rippled through her. Fargo lapped eagerly at her wet core as her head thrashed back and forth on the pillow.

Her climax gradually diminished, and her thighs fell open again. Fargo was able to draw a deep breath at last, the scent of her musk filling his senses.

"Oh, Skye," she whispered. "I never . . . I never dreamed . . . come here."

Fargo slid up beside her and put his arms around her. They kissed, deep and longing, their tongues dueling and dancing sensuously. Diane clasping his manhood again, squeezing it hard.

"It's your turn now," she said after a moment.

She twisted so that she knelt beside him, and when she bent over his midsection the burgeoning pole of male flesh was right in her face. Her long black hair brushed his bare belly, tickling and exciting him at the same time. He felt the warmth of her breath on the head of his shaft and it throbbed in response.

Wrapping her fingers around his manhood to steady it, she began to lick, running her tongue all around the crown. With her other hand she reached down to the heavy sacs at the base of his member and cupped them, rolling them back and forth in the warmth of her palm. She milked beads of moisture from the opening at the tip of his shaft and licked them up. Fargo bit back the groan that tried to come from deep inside him and well up his throat.

Diane made love to him with her mouth and raised him to dizzying heights of passion. When her lips closed around him and she began to suck gently, he thought he was going to spend in her mouth. He held off only with the greatest of efforts. Diane was quite skilled, too, at taking him right to the brink and then drawing back. Fargo was filled with some of the most exquisite sensations he had ever known.

He lost track of time and had no idea how long she had been carrying out this delicious torture on him. But at last she lifted her head from his groin and turned around rapidly, straddling his hips. She sank onto him, grasping his shaft and guiding it unerringly to the opening between her legs. They were both very wet, and he went into her with great ease. He thrust up, she thrust down, and both of them gasped as he penetrated her fully, sheathing all of his organ inside her.

Fargo let her ride him for a few minutes, her hips pumping back and forth as she rested her hands on his chest. He filled his hands with her breasts, cupping them and squeezing them and thumbing the nipples. Diane panted with desire.

Lowering his hands to her hips, Fargo got a good grip on them. He didn't warn her what he was about to do. He just did it, suddenly rolling her over onto her back. His shaft stayed buried in her the whole time. When she was flat on her back she gasped, "Hard now, Skye! Do it to me hard!"

Fargo reached behind him, grasped her ankles, and lifted them so that her legs rested on his shoulders. Poised that way, he could delve deeper into her than ever before. He began thrusting, his hips pistoning back and forth as his pace increased until he was driving deep and hard inside her. It was a good thing he had lived an active life, he thought fleetingly before he gave himself over completely to the sensations filling him. Otherwise this might have killed him.

He called on his great strength and stamina and made love to her that way for long minutes. She climaxed twice more as he drove the great goad of his sex deep inside her, and then a third time as his own culmination gripped him and sent his seed cascading out of him into her. Great shudders shook him as his hips jabbed forward a final few times. He had poured himself out, and she had taken all he had to give her.

Fargo let her legs down but remained inside her, propping himself up on knees and elbows so his weight would not crush her. He leaned down and kissed her lips, her nose, her forehead. Diane wrapped her arms around his neck and hugged him tightly. "You don't know how much that meant to me, Skye," she whispered in his ear.

"It meant an awful lot to me, too," he told her honestly. Even though he wasn't the settling down and marrying kind—at least not at this point in his life— he genuinely loved women, and the times he spent with them like this were as necessary to him as air and water and food. These moments of passion and tenderness revitalized a soul that had seen too much violence and ugliness in its time. Fargo had to be reminded that beauty and love still existed.

When his shaft finally softened enough to slip out of her, he rolled onto his side and she snuggled against him. Fargo put an arm around her and held her close, using his other hand to stroke her hair. He felt a wonderful lassitude stealing over him and knew he was on the verge of falling asleep.

"I'd better go—" he began.

Diane held on to him even tighter. "No! Stay here tonight, Skye. It's all right."

"Your brother—"

"Tom and I are both adults, and he knows that as well as I do. He won't be upset."

Fargo wasn't sure about that. It was a brother's natural instinct to protect his sister. But Diane knew Tom better than he did, Fargo supposed. Anyway, he could sleep a while, then slip out later and return to the professor's wagon. Diane wouldn't have to know about it until morning. . . .

He dozed off, and although he couldn't be sure, he would have sworn that one of the last things he heard as awareness faded away was the distant rumble of thunder.

"Skye! Skye, wake up!"

He came awake instantly, with all of his frontiersman's instincts kicking in, and as he lunged up from the pillows his hand closed around the butt of the Colt he had left on the little table beside the bed.

Diane gave a cry of alarm and jumped back as if Fargo meant to attack her. "Skye, it's me!" she said.

Fargo knew that. His eyes were scanning the rest of the room for trouble. He saw to his surprise that morning sunlight was slanting in through the curtains.

He had slept the night through. This town living was making him lazy.

But he could worry about that later. For now he had more pressing problems. "Diane, what's wrong?" he asked.

She stood there wrapped in a silk robe that was tightly belted around her waist. A worried frown was on her face. "It's Tom," she said. "He's not here."

"Is he supposed to be?"

"No, I mean he hasn't been here. His bed wasn't slept in last night."

"Maybe he just got up early and made it before he went somewhere."

Diane shook her head. "You don't know my brother. He's never made a bed in his life. It's just the way it was after I tended to it yesterday morning."

Fargo lowered the gun, more at ease now that he knew there was no immediate threat. "Maybe Tom spent the night somewhere else," he suggested. "Does he have a special lady friend, maybe, or—"

Again Diane shook her head, even more emphatically this time. "Tom's not romantically involved with anyone right now, at least not that I know of. He puts all of his time and effort into the *Clarion*."

"Can you tell if he's been in the office?"

"I didn't see any signs of it if he has." Diane began to pace back and forth worriedly. "He wasn't even here last night. When we were being careful not to make too much noise, it didn't even matter. He wasn't around to hear us."

Fargo stood up, slipped the Colt back in its holster, and took hold of Diane's shoulders, stopping her anxious pacing.

"Getting yourself all worked up into a state isn't going to help matters," he told her. "If there's no woman in Tom's life, does he have any friends where he might have spent the night? Maybe he started drinking or playing poker with somebody, and the time just got away from him. . . ."

"No," Diane said. "He doesn't do anything like that. I told you, he's devoted to the paper."

"All right. I believe you." Fargo reached for his clothes. "Why don't you get dressed? We'll go out and find him. Topeka's not such a big place that we can't figure out where he is."

But over the next couple of hours Fargo began to wonder if he was right about that. He couldn't find hide nor hair of Thomas Ainsley, nor had anyone seen him since the previous evening. Sheriff Tucker joined the search but didn't have any more luck than Fargo and Diane. Professor Spaulding would have helped, but as he explained it, "Today is the most crucial day yet in my efforts to bring blessed relief to this parched landscape. Before this afternoon is over, rain will have come back to Topeka!"

Fargo could almost believe that when he glanced at the sky and saw the thick gray clouds that were gathering. The overcast was almost complete by noon, with only small gaps here and there where the sun shone through. Spaulding seemed quite pleased with the way things were progressing. He fired off rockets, much to the delight of the crowd, and sent even more smoke and steam rising into the sky. Once an hour, on the hour, he fired off the cannon. That brought more whoops and cheers and applause. The professor rubbed his hands together and continued his spiel nonstop.

Diane was on the verge of hysterics. Fargo wouldn't have believed that her brother could just disappear like this, but he didn't have any explanation for it.

He sent Diane back to the *Clarion* office with the sheriff, asking Tucker to keep her as calm as he could.

Quietly, so that Diane wouldn't overhear, the lawman asked, "What do you plan to do now, Fargo?"

"There's one place in town we haven't checked," Fargo frowned as he looked toward the Grand Kansas Saloon. "Actually, come to think of it, there are three."

"Coleman's saloon and them two warehouses," Tucker guessed.

Fargo nodded. "It seemed so unlikely that Tom would go there I guess I just didn't think of it."

"Tom and Coleman are bitter enemies. I can't see Tom havin' anything to do with Coleman, Brinker, or any o' that bunch."

"Maybe he didn't have any choice in the matter," Fargo said.

Tucker's homely face tightened in anger. "By gum, you're right! Coleman could've decided he wanted to get Tom out of the way."

"Take care of Diane," Fargo said. "Don't let her out of your sight. If Coleman is behind Tom's disappearance, he might not stop there."

The lawman nodded and hurried after Diane, taking her arm and steering her toward the sheriff's office.

Fargo strode deliberately toward the saloon. Several of Brinker's men were on the boardwalk in front, as usual. As he approached, he saw the gunmen stiffen and move toward the door to block his path.

"If you're thinking about getting in my way, boys, you'd better think twice," Fargo said as he stepped up onto the boardwalk, his voice as cold and hard as flint.

"Think twice about what?" one of the gun-hung hardcases asked with a sneer.

"Dying," the Trailsman said.

The gunman's face paled slightly, whether from

anger or fear—or a little bit of both—Fargo didn't know and didn't care. After a moment, the men stepped aside, and he entered the saloon.

As they closed in behind him he felt a crawling sensation on the back of his neck. He was setting himself up for trouble, no doubt about that, but he thought that he could handle whatever came.

Henry Coleman stood at the bar, a drink in his hand. He raised an eyebrow in surprise when he saw Fargo coming toward him.

"This is an unexpected pleasure, Mr. Fargo," he said. "Have you reconsidered my offer and decided to throw your lot in with mine?"

"Not hardly," Fargo grated. "I'm looking for Tom Ainsley."

Coleman threw back the drink. As he placed the empty glass on the bar he asked, "Why come to me? Ainsley and I are hardly friends."

"I thought you might know where he was."

Coleman shook his head. "I haven't seen him."

"You won't mind if I take a look around, then?" Fargo asked.

Coleman waved a slim, elegant hand and said, "Feel free. I have nothing to hide."

That probably meant Ainsley wasn't here, Fargo thought, but it didn't necessarily mean that Coleman didn't know where he was. Still, Fargo thought it best to go ahead and search the saloon, just in case Coleman was bluffing.

Coleman and his hired guns watched as Fargo looked around, including in the rooms off the hall that ran to the rear of the building. The soiled doves who worked in the saloon plied their trade back there. None had customers at the moment. Most were asleep, though one nude, fleshy blonde was sitting in front of a dressing table brushing her hair. She smiled invitingly at Fargo, who nodded, said, "Sorry for the intrusion, ma'am," and backed out of the room.

"Come back any time, cowboy," she called mockingly after him.

Fargo didn't find any sign of Ainsley anywhere in the saloon. Neither did he see Jed Brinker, and that added to his suspicions. It was possible that Brinker was with Ainsley, and that the newspaperman was stashed away somewhere out of the way . . . like in one of the warehouses.

"Satisfied now?" Coleman asked as Fargo returned to the saloon's main room.

"I reckon," Fargo said. "If you see Ainsley, tell him I'm looking for him."

"I doubt very seriously that Thomas Ainsley would set foot in this place."

"Well, just in case he does," Fargo said. He went out, still acutely aware of the hostile stares being directed at his back.

A breeze hit him in the face as he stepped onto the boardwalk, and it carried the faint but unmistakable tang of rain. Fargo looked up at the sky. The clouds were thicker and darker now.

Was it possible? Was the professor actually going to make it rain?

Fargo headed for the end of town opposite the warehouses owned by Coleman. Those warehouses were his ultimate destination, but he intended to circle around and approach them unseen.

As he worked his way around the town he became aware that someone was trailing him. A couple of casual glances over his shoulder revealed the identity of the follower. He was one of Coleman's hired gun-throwers, and although he tried to look like he had no interest in the Trailsman, Fargo knew better.

He headed down an alley, knowing that the hard-case would follow. He went around a corner, saw a rain barrel sitting there—unused in recent months, but maybe that would change today—and lithely stepped up onto it. He reached up, grasped the edge of the roof over his head, and pulled himself up, rolling away from the edge to avoid being seen. He heard rapid footsteps in the dust below.

The gunman stopped almost directly underneath. He looked around worriedly and muttered under his breath, "Where the hell'd he go?"

A minute later a second man joined the first. "Where's Fargo?" the second man demanded. "You were supposed to be keeping an eye on him."

"I was! The son of a bitch up and vanished on me."

"Nobody vanishes into thin air," the second man said. "He's got to be around here somewhere."

"Well, he ain't. He came around this corner, and that was the last I saw of him. There's no doors he could have ducked into, and I would have seen him if he was still outside."

"Coleman'll have your hide. He doesn't want Fargo getting anywhere near that warehouse where he's got Ainsley stashed."

"Yeah, I know he don't want Ainsley gettin' loose and warnin' those damn townies about the blockade."

Blockade? That was something new.

The second man chuckled. "The whole town'll fall in line quick enough when they realize nothing's getting in or out on the roads without our say-so. Then they'll stop bitching about the boss's prices and pay whatever they're told to. They won't dare try to arrest him, either."

"And when they can't pay up, he'll take their places and wind up ownin' the whole town. Coleman's a devious rascal, that's for sure."

"Yeah, as long as Fargo doesn't ruin everything." The second man took his hat off and scratched his head. "I'd sure like to know where he went. It's almost like he grew wings and flew away. . . ."

That thought made the man tip his head back and look up. Fargo was ready for that. As the gunman's eyes spotted him on the roof and widened in shock, Fargo gathered his muscles and launched himself into the air.

10

Spreading out on the way down, Fargo was able to drive his feet into the chest of one man while tackling the other and bearing him to the ground. The man he had kicked sailed backward and landed heavily. The crash of his coming back to earth knocked all the air out of his lungs and left him stunned and gasping.

Fargo landed on top of the other man. He brought both knees up into the hardcase's belly and then, poised there, slammed a right and a left into the man's face. The second blow knocked him cold.

Rolling off his opponent and surging back to his feet, Fargo saw the remaining gunman struggling upright. A quick step brought Fargo to him, and a looping right fist exploded on the man's jaw, sending him down and out.

Fargo's hat had flown off during his dive from the roof. He picked it up, knocked some of the dust off it, and settled it on his head again as he caught his breath. Using the belts from the unconscious men, he tied their hands and then stuffed their bandannas in their mouths. That wouldn't keep them quiet and still for long, but maybe he wouldn't need that much time to find Tom Ainsley.

The wheels of Fargo's brain spun rapidly as he hurried toward Coleman's warehouses. Judging by what he had overheard, Coleman had gotten hold of Ainsley and found out that the law planned to move against him as soon as the fair was over. Coleman was going to strike first, throwing a blockade of hired killers around the town so that Topeka would be cut off from the outside world. That meant no supplies at all coming in, and with that hammer to hold over the heads of the citizens, they would have to give Coleman whatever he wanted.

On the face of it, none of Coleman's claims would stand up in a court of law. Fargo was enough of a realist, though, to know that possession was truly nine-tenths of the law, especially on the frontier. Like it or not, a man with enough money and power was beyond the reach of the judicial system, and Henry Coleman was well on his way to having that much money and power.

Soon the law might not be able to touch Coleman, but justice still could—the justice that a man held in his fist.

As Fargo reached the back of one of Coleman's warehouses, something struck his cheek. It took a second for him to realize what it was, but as moisture ran down through his closely cropped beard to his chin, he knew it was beginning to rain. He paused for a second and watched big fat drops plop down in the dust of the alley. There were only a few of them, and they were widely spaced, but it was a start.

Out on the street, Professor Spaulding's cannon went off again, and folks cheered. Soon they would really have something to cheer about . . . but not unless they could break the stranglehold that Coleman had on the town.

This was the same warehouse Fargo had broken into earlier. The back door had been secured by a padlock. Fargo didn't know how he was going to get past it, but then lightning flickered overhead and a second later thunder boomed loudly. Thunderstorms were rare on the plains at this time of year, but obviously, that was what the professor had conjured up. Fargo slipped his Colt from its holster and waited.

A moment later lightning flashed again. He timed his shot to coincide with the huge clap of thunder that followed. The rolling explosion of sound from above was so loud that no one inside the warehouse could have heard the shot. He jerked at the bullet-mangled padlock and slipped it from the hasp. He pulled the door open.

Fargo slipped inside, gun in hand, and moved rapidly through the empty office and into the main part of the building. He eased through the door into the labyrinth of boxes and crates and barrels. The sound of voices led him toward the front of the building.

Thunder rumbled again. Fargo heard rain hitting the roof. He didn't know if the storm's arrival was merely a coincidence, or if Professor Spaulding really had something to do with it. At this point, it didn't matter. Even through the thick walls of the warehouse, Fargo could hear the celebration going on outside as the townspeople and the farmers who had come in for the fair welcomed the much-needed rain.

"Damn it!" Jed Brinker said. "Who'd have thought that crazy old goat could really make it rain?"

"Coleman's plans are ruined now." The thin, weak voice belonged to Thomas Ainsley. "The drought is over, and Coleman will be going to jail along with you and the rest of your gunnies."

"Not so fast," Brinker said, a sneer in his tone. "It's barely started raining. There may not be enough to even get the top of the ground good and wet. And as for Coleman going to jail, that ain't likely to happen. You ruined that by barging into the Grand Kansas to gloat about what Fargo found in here."

Fargo's jaw tightened. So Ainsley had put himself in Coleman's hands, and not only that, he had also tipped off Coleman what Fargo and Sheriff Tucker were planning. Whatever had possessed him to do a thing like that?

But even as the question went through Fargo's mind, he thought he might know the answer. Ainsley had taken quite a few bad blows to the head during that beating, and then instead of resting as the doctor told him to, he had pushed himself even harder as he worked on the newspaper. Fargo had seen cases of head injuries like that causing a man to get all addled in his thinking. Because of that Ainsley could have believed he was doing the right thing by confronting Coleman, even though normally he never would have done such a thing.

Maybe they could figure that out later, Fargo told himself. Right now the most important thing was to free Ainsley from captivity and then go ahead and move against Coleman. There was no point in waiting now. Delaying the showdown would just allow Coleman to seize the advantage.

Fargo listened carefully, but no one seemed to be guarding Ainsley except Jed Brinker. With his Colt gripped firmly in his hand, the Trailsman stepped around the last stack of crates and pointed the revolver at Brinker, who sat on a box next to Ainsley. The newspaperman was tied up and lying uncomfortably on the floor.

"Hold it, Brinker!" Fargo snapped. "Don't make a move."

Brinker came halfway up in a crouch, his face twisting in a hate-filled grimace as he instinctively reached for his gun. He froze, though, with his hand still several inches away from the butt of the weapon.

"Fargo!" he hissed as he stared down the barrel of the Colt.

"That's right. Keep your hand away from your gun and move away from Ainsley."

"Mr. Fargo!" Ainsley exclaimed. "I'm sorry, I don't know what I was doing, I was out of my head and I went into the saloon and started babbling about our plans—"

"Take it easy, Tom," Fargo told him, trying to calm him. "Something went a little wrong in your head, that's all. You'll be fine once this is over and you get a chance to rest up."

"It'll be a long rest," Brinker sneered, "because you'll all be dead!"

"Shut up," Fargo said. "Now move back, like I said."

Brinker took a reluctant step back, which put him next to a stack of crates. Suddenly, without warning he lunged into the crates, lowering his shoulder and shoving. Fargo snapped a shot at him, but the bullet thudded into one of the sliding boxes. The whole stack began to topple toward the helpless Tom Ainsley.

Fargo flung himself forward, reached down to grab Ainsley's shirt, and threw himself out of the way of the falling crates. Fargo hauled him out of the way just as the boxes smashed onto the floor.

Brinker's gun blasted, the report echoing hollowly from the high ceiling of the warehouse. The bullet plowed into the planks of the floor only a few inches from Fargo's head.

Fargo rolled, taking the tied-up Ainsley with him. He shoved the helpless newspaperman into a little alcove between two barrels. He leaped to his feet and tried to locate Brinker.

The gunman fired again, and this time Fargo felt as

much as heard the wind-rip of the slug's passage beside his ear. He caught a glimpse of the muzzle flash and fired back. Another shot answered his own.

Fargo crouched behind a crate and listened. He heard the thunder, the cheers of the crowd outside, the pelting sound of a hard rain hitting the roof of the warehouse. But he didn't hear what he was listening for, which was the sound of Brinker moving.

Tense moments ticked by. Fargo waited, knowing that the first man who moved in this deadly cat-and-mouse game would probably be the loser. And losing meant dying.

Brinker's patience snapped before Fargo's did, but Fargo had to give him credit for doing the unexpected. Brinker climbed onto the crates and came leaping from stack to stack, toppling crates behind him. The gun in his hand spouted flame and lead as he fired down at Fargo.

At the last second, Fargo threw himself aside, rolled over, and fired up at Brinker. The heavy slug caught the gunman in midair and knocked him into a twisting, spinning fall. Brinker yelled and grabbed at the edge of a crate, trying to stop his plunge, but all he succeeded in doing was pulling the crate over on top of him. It crashed down, cutting off Brinker's scream and landing on his head with a soggy thud.

Fargo covered Brinker, but he could tell by the blood that ran out from under the fallen crate and the fading twitches in the man's body that Brinker was no longer a threat. The sight made a sour taste well up in Fargo's throat. Brinker had been a gunman and a killer, but that was still a bad way to die.

When he was satisfied that Brinker was dead, Fargo hurried over to Ainsley and knelt beside him. The Arkansas Toothpick flashed in the lamplight as Fargo cut the bonds on the newspaperman's wrists and ankles. Ainsley gasped in mingled relief and pain as feeling began to flood back into his extremities.

"I'm sorry, Mr. Fargo," he said. "And I was never so glad to see anybody in my life as when you stepped around those crates."

"Don't worry about that now," Fargo told him. "In a minute or two you'll be able to walk. When you can, go out the back and head for the *Clarion* office as fast as you can get there. Your sister and the sheriff ought to be there. If they're not, look around until you find them. Tell them we have to move against Coleman now."

Ainsley nodded. "Is . . . is it really raining out there?"

Fargo allowed himself a brief smile. "It's really raining. Don't know how long it'll last, though." He straightened to his feet. "Remember, find the sheriff. And if you see any of the other men who were going to be with us in the fight, warn them, too."

"I'll do it," Ainsley promised. "What are you going to do?"

"Beard the lion in his den," Fargo said. "I'll try to keep Coleman and his men busy so they can't get out of town and blockade the roads."

He hurried out of the warehouse, leaving Ainsley rubbing feeling back into his feet and legs.

He stepped out into a driving rain. The broad-brimmed hat kept water from his eyes, but he was soaked by the time he reached the main street. He stepped under the awning over the boardwalk and watched the celebration. People were dancing in the street, heedless of the rain.

Fargo hurried toward the church where Joshua McCabe's wagons were parked. Over the past three days of the fair, all the supplies had been handed out in as fair and equitable a fashion as McCabe could manage. Soon he and Sallie and the others would be starting back, and from the looks of this rain, there wouldn't be any need for them to make a return trip.

"Brother Fargo!" McCabe called from the door of the church, waving to Fargo as he spotted him. Fargo trotted over to the sanctuary and went inside, finding that McCabe, Sallie, Reuben Sanborn, and the rest of the party had taken shelter from the storm inside the church.

Sallie threw her arms around him and hugged him excitedly, ignoring Fargo's soaking wet buckskins. "Isn't it wonderful, Skye?" she asked. "The professor really made it rain!"

"The Good Lord made it rain, Sallie," her father corrected. A grin stretched across McCabe's face. "But I reckon maybe Professor Spaulding gave Him a hand."

Reuben knew Fargo better than the McCabes did. He saw the look on the Trailsman's face. "What's wrong, Skye?"

"Coleman's going to try to take over the town today," Fargo replied. "He's going to send his gunmen out to blockade all the roads."

"Why, he can't do that!" McCabe exclaimed. "We have to get back home."

"He plans to bottle up everybody and keep the town shut off until everything belongs to him. He'll starve people into signing over their homes and businesses to him, I imagine."

Sallie said, "He can't get away with that!"

"The army'll come in and put a stop to it," Reuben declared.

Fargo shook his head. "Not until Coleman's looted the whole place. And he's liable to make it look just legal enough to get by."

"We got to stop him," McCabe said.

"I'm on my way to the saloon now."

"I'm going with you," Reuben said.

"No!" Sallie cried. "You're not well enough yet."

"I can walk and fire a gun," Reuben replied stubbornly. "That's all I need to do."

McCabe uncoiled his bullwhip and let it writhe around his feet. "I'm with you, too, Brother Fargo. We'll root out those evildoers."

Several other men inside the church called out their agreement. Fargo looked around at their grim faces and nodded. "Let's go."

"Well, then, I'm coming, too!" Sallie drew the holstered pistol at her waist. "I'm as good a shot as anybody here."

"You've always been a vexatious child with a mind of your own," her father said. "I don't suppose it would do any good to argue with you."

"Not a blessed bit."

Fargo reloaded his Colt, replacing the rounds that had gotten damp in the rain and the ones he had emptied in the warehouse during the fight with Brinker. "Keep your powder as dry as you can," he warned the others as they left the church. "You won't be able to afford many misfires."

He tucked the Colt behind his belt and draped his shirt over it, rather than holstering it normally. The others followed suit. With a force of about fifteen men—plus Sallie—behind him, Fargo started for the Grand Kansas Saloon.

"Tom Ainsley is trying to round up the sheriff and some other men," he said as they made their way along the street.

"You found Ainsley, then?" Reuben asked.

Fargo nodded grimly. "Coleman was holding him prisoner in one of those warehouses." He didn't add that Ainsley had gotten himself into that mess because of his muddled brain. That could all be hashed out later.

The rain had let up a little, but it still fell steadily. The street was crowded. For all practical purposes, the fair was over. It had culminated with the onset of the rainstorm. But people were still celebrating and likely would long into the night.

Fargo saw Sheriff Tucker and several men coming the other way along the street, staying under the boardwalk as they marched toward the saloon. Tucker was carrying a shotgun and looked fierce and grim, and Fargo knew that Ainsley had reached the sheriff and passed along Fargo's message.

The two groups met across the street from the Grand Kansas. "What do you reckon we ought to do now, Fargo?" Tucker asked. "Go over there and bust right into that nest o' snakes?"

Fargo nodded. "No point in wasting time." He had been prepared to carry the fight to Coleman alone, but that wasn't going to be necessary. "Keep your powder dry," he said again as he stepped out into the street.

Another peal of thunder rolled through the heavens at that moment, so Fargo couldn't hear the glass shattering as somebody knocked out one of the saloon's front windows from inside. But he saw the sudden spray of shards and the rifle barrel that poked through the opening.

"Get back!" Fargo bellowed as the rifleman inside the saloon opened fire.

More windows were broken out, and a fusillade of lead raked the mud around Fargo. They dived for cover, some men throwing themselves behind water troughs and rain barrels while others retreated into the building behind them. Fargo knew some had been hit—he had heard the whine of bullets past his own head—but no one had been killed so far. They began returning the fire from inside the saloon.

He knelt behind a barrel on the boardwalk and leveled his Colt, squeezing off shot after steady shot. He hoped all the innocent bystanders inside the saloon, if there were any, had either gotten out the back or were keeping their heads down. Coleman had started this fight, though, when he saw the armed group closing in on him. The blood was on his hands.

For long minutes the two sides poured deadly gunfire at each other. Bullets chewed up the front of the saloon as well as the building where Fargo's bunch had taken cover. The gray, rainy day was brightened by hundreds of muzzle flashes that rivaled the lightning still flickering overhead.

The rain barrel Fargo was using for cover was getting shot to pieces and wouldn't be much good for much longer. He turned and dove for the door of the building, lead plucking at the sleeve of his shirt. He sailed through the open door and slid for a few feet, then rolled to the side as bullets smacked into the floor. He saw that he and the others had taken refuge inside a saddle shop. The smell of leather probably would have been pleasant had it not been mixed with the acrid tang of powder smoke.

Reuben, Sallie, McCabe, and Sheriff Tucker crouched at the front windows, keeping up the fire toward the saloon. The big mountain man glanced over his shoulder and said over the roar of the shots, "It's gonna be hard to pry them out of there, Skye!"

Fargo knew that was true. He had hoped to pounce on Coleman and his hired guns before they could fort up inside the saloon, but it hadn't worked out that way.

"We've got several men who're wounded," Tucker said. "There are at least twenty hardcases over there, more than likely. If we go at 'em straight on, they'll wipe us out."

"We won't do that," Fargo said. An idea was beginning to form in his mind. "At least not until we've softened them up a little first."

"What are you thinking about, Skye?" Reuben asked.

Fargo reloaded his gun and slipped it behind his belt again. "Keep them pinned down for a few minutes," he said. "I'll be back."

"We'll keep 'em pinned down, all right," muttered the sheriff. "Or they'll keep us pinned down, whichever."

Fargo ducked out the back door of the saddle shop and ran along the rear alley. When he reached the end of the block he circled the buildings and found himself close by Professor Spaulding's wagon, as he had planned. Everybody had cleared out due to the battle up the street, but the professor himself was still there, peeking out nervously from the back of the wagon.

Hoping that none of Coleman's bunch would see him through the pouring rain, Fargo darted across to the wagon and leaped up onto the driver's box. He opened the door and found the professor inside, huddled amidst all the rainmaking equipment.

"Professor," Fargo said urgently, "are you all right?"

"Fit as a fiddle, my boy, fit as a fiddle," Spaulding replied. He looked scared, though. But at the same time there was pride on his face. "You see the rain? You see that I delivered on my promise to produce precipitation?"

"I sure do, Professor. Nobody could miss that downpour. Where are your horses?"

Spaulding frowned in puzzlement. "Why, they're in the stable right next door."

"Let's get them hitched up."

"Hitched up?" the professor repeated. "But where are we going?"

"To war," Fargo said.

It didn't take long to lead out the horses and get them hitched to the wagon, even though the weather made them somewhat uncooperative. The gunfight up the street continued, and Fargo hoped that none of his friends had been wounded or killed while he was down here wrestling with the professor's team. If his plan worked, though, it would be the quickest way to bring this battle to a halt.

When the wagon was ready, Fargo took up the reins and called, "Hang on, Professor!" He whipped the horses into motion and sent the wagon careening around the buildings. A couple of bullets thudded into the back of the vehicle as he drove, and Fargo knew somebody inside the saloon had finally spotted him down here. He just hoped they hadn't figured out what he was up to.

Spaulding let out an involuntary cry as the wagon jolted and lurched along the rough alley. Fargo hauled back on the reins, bringing it to a stop behind the saddle shop. He leaped down from the box and hurried inside. Relief touched him when he saw that Sallie, Reuben, McCabe, and Tucker all were unharmed. One man was dead, though, shot through the head, and several others were badly injured. Fargo's mouth tightened into a grim slash.

"Three of you men give me a hand," he said. He had already explained the professor's part in this campaign, and Spaulding was hurrying in with the rocket-launching tube in his arms, along with some rockets. Spaulding set up the launcher while Fargo and several other men carried the cannon from the wagon

151

through the back door of the shop. They set it down so that it wasn't visible through the open front door.

"As I told you, Mr. Fargo, I don't have any regular cannonballs," the professor said. "I assure you, however, that the charges I use to disperse the necessary ingredients into the clouds will produce quite a potent detonation."

"I believe you, Professor. Go to it."

Spaulding loaded the cannon with an oblong shell he brought from the wagon, ramming home a charge of powder down the barrel first.

"Is the first rocket ready?" Fargo asked.

"Yes, all Mr. Sanborn has to do is light the fuse."

Reuben grinned at Fargo around the lit cigar he now had clenched between his teeth.

Fargo nodded and said, "Let's do it."

He and a couple of other men grabbed the cannon and rolled it into place. They ducked back as some of Coleman's gunmen spotted them in the opening and took potshots at them. Crouching low, Fargo reached out, grasped the firing lanyard attached to the cannon, and gave it a good swift yank, activating the friction trigger.

The powder charge went off with a roar and sent the cannon rolling backward on the wheels of its carriage. "Light the rocket!" Fargo called to Reuben.

Across the street the shell crashed into the front doors of the Grand Kansas Saloon and blew them clear off their hinges. It burst a second later in a shattering explosion. Right on its heels came the sputtering, blazing rocket, and already Spaulding was loading another one into the tube. Reuben touched off the fuse with his cigar and sent the rocket screaming across the street into the saloon.

Smoke billowed out through the broken windows. Flames flickered garishly inside. Fire was one of the most feared calamities on the frontier—it could spread so easily from building to building and burn an entire town to the ground. Not in the middle of a rainstorm like this, though. The blaze would be confined to the saloon.

Some of the gunmen inside stumbled out with their hands up. Others still tried to shoot it out, but with their eyes streaming tears from the smoke, they couldn't see to aim. They were cut down, most of them fatally, by Fargo and his friends.

So far, Fargo hadn't seen Henry Coleman come out of the saloon. He waited, hoping to get a shot at the mastermind behind all of Topeka's troubles. Still Coleman didn't emerge.

"Skye! Skye!"

The voice screaming his name belonged to Diane Ainsley, Fargo realized as horror went through him. Ignoring the possible danger, he ran out onto the boardwalk and looked toward the *Clarion* office. Coleman had come out of the office with his left arm around Diane's throat, dragging her along with him. His right hand held a gun pressed to her head.

Fargo knew that Coleman must have slipped out the back of the saloon before the cannon and the rockets blasted the place. Realizing the game was over, Coleman had made it to the newspaper and seized a hostage.

"Fargo!" Coleman yelled. "Fargo, come out where I can kill you!"

"I'm here," Fargo called as he stepped out farther on the boardwalk.

From behind him, Sallie McCabe screamed, "Skye, don't go out there. He's crazy!"

"Let him alone," Reuben rumbled. "Ol' Skye knows what he's doing."

Fargo stepped into the street, letting the rain pelt

his muddy buckskins. He walked steadily toward Coleman and Diane.

"Skye," she sobbed past the arm pressed across her throat, "he shot Tom!"

"Ainsley got what was coming to him," Coleman snapped. "He got in my way. Anyone who interferes with me deserves to die!"

Coleman had come a little unhinged, Fargo decided, and that made him even more deadly.

When only ten feet separated them, Coleman took the gun away from Diane's head and pointed it at Fargo. "Drop your gun!" he ordered.

"Sure," Fargo said. "Just don't get trigger-happy, Coleman." He reached slowly under his shirt and took the Colt from behind his belt. Bending at the knees, he leaned down to place the gun on the ground.

Coleman didn't wait for Fargo to straighten. He pulled the trigger.

The pistol clicked but didn't fire. The rain had dampened the powder too much, as Fargo had known it would.

Realizing that Coleman's gun was useless, Diane drove an elbow back into the man's midsection and tore loose from his grip. She threw herself to the side as Fargo came up out of his crouch. The Arkansas Toothpick slid out of its sheath.

Coleman threw the pistol aside and snapped his wrist. A derringer, a gambler's hide-out gun, leaped from its spring-loaded holster under his sleeve into his hand. This weapon, having been protected from the rain, would work just fine.

Fargo's knife flashed through the rain as Coleman pulled the trigger and the derringer went off with a wicked crack. The bullet whipped past Fargo's head. Coleman staggered back a step and stared down in horror at the blade buried in his chest.

His eyes rolled up in his head and he collapsed, falling in the mud. The great rainstorm that would be famous in years to come for breaking the terrible drought in Kansas Territory pounded down on him, washing away the blood that welled out around the Arkansas Toothpick.

Fargo went to Diane and lifted her to her feet. She held tightly to him, whispering, "Thank God, thank God . . ."

Sheriff Tucker came up beside them and looked down at Coleman's body. "Damn fool should have had sense enough to know when to give up." The lawman paused and then added, "Reckon I'm glad he didn't, though."

Coleman had wounded Thomas Ainsley when he burst into the newspaper office, but the doctor said that Ainsley likely would live.

"He'll really have to take it easy this time, though," Diane told Fargo that night. "The doctor's going to keep Tom at his place until he's completely recovered."

"That'll leave you to get the paper out by yourself," Fargo said.

"I can do it," she replied confidently.

Fargo smiled. "You know, I believe you can."

They stood on the boardwalk in front of the office, watching the rain fall. It was a steady drizzle now, and although neither of them knew it, it would continue to fall like that for another three days, a deep soaking rain that was exactly what the thirsty landscape needed.

"Are you going back to Missouri with the McCabes and Mr. Sanborn?" Diane asked.

Fargo shook his head. "No, Reuben and Sallie have decided to get married right here in Topeka before they start back. I'll stay long enough to attend the wedding, but then I'm moving on west."

"You never stay in one place for very long, do you, Skye?"

"I never claimed otherwise."

She rested her head on his shoulder, and he slipped an arm around her waist. "I know," she said softly. "And I wouldn't try to hold you. You're like the rain, Skye Fargo. You come into people's lives and then move on, but you leave something behind you."

"Mud?" Fargo asked with a chuckle.

"Hope," Diane said.

They stood there quietly for a few moments, and then Diane asked, "Have you ever made love to the sound of rain hitting the window?"

"I reckon I have."

"So have I. Let's go do it again."

That was the best suggestion Fargo had heard in a long time.

THE TRAILSMAN #283
COLORADO CLAIM JUMPERS

*Denver City, 1858—There's gold in Cherry
Creek if you can hang on to your claim—
something that's not easy for a dead man to do.*

Afterward, the man with the lake-blue eyes couldn't
have said exactly what it was that warned him.

It might have been some sound that he didn't even
know he'd heard.

It might have been the absence of sound, the sudden
end of birds calling and fluttering or of squirrels
chattering.

It might even have been nothing more than instinct,
honed and kept sharp by years on the trail when there
was no one but himself to watch his back, front, and
sides.

Whatever it was that warned him, Skye Fargo was
out of the saddle and rolling to one side when he

heard the bullet smack into the pine tree that was now in front of him. And by the time the sound of the shot had followed the bullet, his heavy Colt was already in his hand.

A second bullet thudded into the soft trunk of the pine, sending bark chips flying, and Fargo's big Ovaro stallion, who was smarter than some humans Fargo had known, wandered off into the brush where he couldn't be easily seen.

Fargo was glad the horse was well hidden, but the trouble was that his attacker couldn't be easily seen, either. Fargo let his eyes roam over the intense green of the surrounding pines. There was no sign of a shooter, but there were plenty of places he could be hiding.

Fargo sighed. It was too nice a day to have to deal with bushwhackers. The sun was shining up in the blue sky, and the smell of the pines was strong and sweet.

A bullet chipped off a limb above Fargo's head, and he looked across the trail to a wide place a good way up ahead, where a rocky outcropping jutted from a thin line of cedars. Fargo thought he saw a thin gray haze of gun smoke slowly rising above the cedars, but he could have been imagining it. So he lay there, listening to the unnatural quiet, and waited.

No more shots were fired, and after a few minutes the familiar sounds began to return. A couple of squirrels started up an argument over who had the right of way on a limb, a woodpecker began hammering at a tree trunk, and something moved heavily back in the brush. Not a man, Fargo thought. Most likely it was the Ovaro, though it might be a bear. It was late enough in the spring for bears to be out and roaming around, so Fargo took a look around. He caught a glimpse of the Ovaro and turned back to look at the outcropping again.

There was no movement, and Fargo wondered who had taken a shot at him. He knew that whoever it was hadn't followed him from Kansas. He'd crossed too much open ground for anyone to follow him unnoticed, and even if he'd been in a thicket, he'd have known if anyone had been behind him. If Fargo knew anything at all, he knew about finding his way from one place to another, and about spotting anyone who might be tracking him.

Nobody had been. He was sure of that much, which meant that someone had been waiting for him. He wondered why, and he wondered how they'd known where he'd be. There were plenty of people who'd wanted him dead at one time or another, so many that Fargo had pretty much lost count, but he didn't think any of that bunch would know where he happened to be at this particular time.

He wondered how many shooters were hiding out there. Could be only one, he thought. An ambush didn't require any more than that. But he was pretty sure there were at least two. The second shot had come too soon for it to have been fired from the same rifle as the first, unless that shooter could reload a Sharps faster than just about anybody Fargo had ever known or heard of.

Fargo wondered if the bushwhackers were as patient as he was. He'd spent most of his life on the trail, in the woods, and under the open sky away from towns and people. He'd learned patience a long time ago.

It could be that whoever had taken the shots at him would think he'd been hit. If that was the case, sooner or later they'd have to come out and see if he was dead—either that or just ride off, thinking that maybe he wouldn't come after them.

He hoped they'd come to check on him. He could ask them all those things he was wondering about, and ask them none too gently, either.

Red Stover leaned back against the smooth rock and spit a stream of tobacco juice on the dirt. "Reckon I got him. Pounded his ass right out of that saddle with the first shot."

"Don't think so," Lett Plunkett said.

Red's beady eyes narrowed. "You sayin' you got him? You thinkin' you'll get more pay if you're the one killed him?"

Lett was tall and wide and looked mean as a grizzly, which he was. But this time he wasn't looking for an argument.

"Ain't sayin' nothin' of the kind, nor lookin' for any extra pay. I'm just sayin' that he's not hit."

"The hell he ain't." Red had the temper that was supposedly typical of all redheads, though his own hair had faded to a peculiar shade of orange. "You saw him fall soon's I shot him. I didn't miss."

Lett's voice remained mild. "Ain't sayin' you missed, and I ain't sayin' he didn't fall."

Red spit again and wiped his mouth with the back of his hand. "You're one agreeable son of a bitch, ain't you," he said.

"Ain't sayin' I agree with you."

"Then what in thunderin' hell *are* you sayin'?"

Lett didn't answer for a few seconds, and a dark flush started to creep up Red's neck and onto his face.

"You slow-talking bastard," Red said. "You tell me

160

what you're thinkin', or by God I'll turn this Sharps on *you*."

"You wouldn't want to do that," Lett said, and Red knew he was right.

In the short time that Red had known Lett, he'd seen the big outlaw kill one man with his bare hands and rip another one from asshole to appetite with the big bowie knife he carried in a scabbard that hung from his belt. No matter how mad he got, Red wasn't going to try anything with Lett.

At least not while Lett could see him. If Lett turned his back, well, that was a whole different story. Red wasn't afraid of anybody who had his back turned.

"I'm just a little nervy, I guess," Red said by way of apology. "But I sure thought I shot that fella."

"He was too fast for us," Lett said. "He fell, all right, but he was already halfway out of the saddle before you pulled the trigger. I don't know what tipped him off, but somehow or other he knew we were here and gunnin' for him."

"No way he could've known," Red said.

"Maybe not. You know what they call him?"

"That fella we're supposed to kill? Yeah. Name's Fargo, but they call him the Trailsman. So what?"

"So he's not as easy to kill as some tenderfoot peckerhead. We should've been more careful."

"Don't think we could've been."

"Maybe not," Lett said. "The thing is, he's still alive, and he's out there waitin' for us to come for him."

"We could fool him," Red said, not liking that idea. "We could get our horses and get out of here."

"Yeah, and not get paid. How would you like that?"

Red admitted that he wouldn't like it one bit. He

wanted the money, as he'd already planned on spending some of it for whiskey and a whore.

"So what're we gonna do?" he asked.

"What the hell do you think?" Lett said. "We're gonna go get him."

Red wasn't so sure he wanted to do that, but he wasn't going to cross Lett. Better the devil you know, he thought, than the devil you don't.

"Where you reckon he is?" he asked.

"Behind that tree where we saw him fall. Unless he's moved, in which case he could be anywhere. What the hell difference does it make?"

It didn't make any difference, and Red knew it. As much as he wanted to get out of there and forget the whole thing, he wanted the money more. And he was more afraid of Lett than any damn Trailsman.

"You got a plan?" Red asked.

"Yeah," Lett said.

"Let's have it then."

So Lett told him what it was.

No other series has this much historical action!

THE TRAILSMAN

#255:	MONTANA MADMEN	0-451-20774-2
#256:	HIGH COUNTRY HORROR	0-451-20805-6
#257:	COLORADO CUTTHROATS	0-451-20827-7
#258:	CASINO CARNAGE	0-451-20839-0
#259:	WYOMING WOLF PACK	0-451-20860-9
#260:	BLOOD WEDDING	0-451-20901-X
#261:	DESERT DEATH TRAP	0-451-20925-7
#262:	BADLAND BLOODBATH	0-451-20952-4
#263:	ARKANSAS ASSAULT	0-451-20966-4
#264:	SNAKE RIVER RUINS	0-451-20999-0
#265:	DAKOTA DEATH RATTLE	0-451-21000-X
#266:	SIX-GUN SCHOLAR	0-451-21001-8
#267:	CALIFORNIA CASUALTIES	0-451-21069-4
#268:	NEW MEXICO NYMPH	0-451-21137-5
#269:	DEVIL'S DEN	0-451-21154-5
#270:	COLORADO CORPSE	0-451-21177-4
#271:	ST. LOUIS SINNERS	0-451-21190-1
#272:	NEVADA NEMESIS	0-451-21256-8
#273:	MONTANA MASSACRE	0-451-21256-8
#274:	NEBRASKA NIGHTMARE	0-451-21273-8
#275:	OZARKS ONSLAUGHT	0-451-21290-8
#276:	SKELETON CANYON	0-451-21338-6
#277:	HELL'S BELLES	0-451-21356-4
#278:	MOUNTAIN MANHUNT	0-451-21373-4
#279:	DEATH VALLEY VENGEANCE	0-451-21385-8
#280:	TEXAS TART	0-451-21433-1
#281:	NEW MEXICO NIGHTMARE	0-451-21453-6

Available wherever books are sold or at
www.penguin.com

S310

Ralph Cotton

THE BIG IRON SERIES

JURISDICTION
0-451-20547-2

Young Arizona Ranger Sam Burrack has vowed to bring
down a posse of murderous outlaws—and save the
impressionable young boy they've befriended.

VENGEANCE IS A BULLET
0-451-20799-8

Arizona Ranger Sam Burrack must hunt down a lethal
killer whose mind is bent by revenge and won't stop killing
until the desert is piled high with the bodies of those
who wronged him.

HELL'S RIDERS
0-451-21186-3

While escorting a prisoner to the county seat, Arizona Ranger
Sam Burrack comes across the victims of a scalp-hunting
party. Once he learns that the brutal outlaws have
kidnapped a young girl, he joins the local sheriff in the
pursuit—dragging along his reluctant captive.

**Available wherever books are sold or at
www.penguin.com**